BEST WOMEN'S EROTICA 2009

BEST WOMEN'S EROTICA 2009

Edited by

VIOLET BLUE

Published in the United States by Cleis Press Inc.,
P.O. Box 14697, San Francisco, California 94114.

Printed in the United States.
Cover design: Scott Idleman
Cover photograph: Christine Kessler
Text design: Frank Wiedemann
Cleis Press logo art: Juana Alicia
First Edition.
10 9 8 7 6 5 4 3 2

For Jonathan

CONTENTS

INTRODUCTION: PERSEPHONE COMES OF AGE

When you're ready, really ready for sex, desire becomes an ache, a throb that pulses with the rhythm of your blood beating in your head and between your legs. You want to peel away the layers obscuring your object of desire until you get to the juicy, sweet fruit within. And when you finally sink your teeth in—the initiation begins.

The only problem, of course, with using a ripening fruit analogy for sexual initiation and Eros' coming of age—when he sits on your chest and plucks at the strings between pussy and heart until you sing with desperate want—is that fruit only ripens once. Yet as desire for the thing we've never had burns through us, consumes us, then somehow, magically, with sex as with nothing else, the cycle begins again. We do not rot, we swell and grow juicy and pick the flower that pulls us into the underworld and we beg Hades for another deflowering. We demand it.

The clocks and calendars conspired against Persephone. She had never intended to spend her afternoons with her virginity clamped furtively between her legs, her mind insanely playing blue movies of hard-core decadence on the screen behind her eyes. Persephone: a girl stuck frolicking in fields of flowers with a bunch of boring maidens who had no fucking idea how good it felt to rub yourself to wet explosion thinking of huge-cocked satyrs, nubile and voluptuous and wet nymphs, costume parties where only masks and eager mouths were required for entry; trapped among idiots staring at flowers all day.

I'm sure Persephone hated being a virgin, forced to navigate her lust with hot and prickly skin, perfecting quiet masturbation, and wandering those damn flower fields with legs rubbery and fingertips shriveled from seeking relief when everyone else was distracted. Imagine the glow she must have had from her third, her fourth clandestine orgasm, when she saw the single narcissus that, according to legend, was glowing as much as she.

The myths portray Persephone as an innocent moth to the flame, lured by Hades (or Pluto), god of the underworld, when he performed a particularly evil bait and switch and the naïve young goddess plucked the flower that would seal her fate and open the world for her to fall into hell, and into Hades' arms.

We all know what it's like to feel the need for fucking and being fucked, remember needing it more than air, for the very first time. Persephone floated awkwardly toward the narcissus, I'm sure, all girlish knobby knees and elbows at angles and ears sticking out and pussy burning as hot as Helios, who, as everyone knows, watched her that day, watched her every day. The flower glowed like the sharp hard-on of her clit, and made of the same stuff, it pulled her like a magnet. And when she crushed the flower to her mouth, squeezing the juice down her chin, destroying the blossom between her breasts as her eyes rolled back in ecstasy and sweet pain and all things sexual, the earth opened up, and she slid home.

When her mother Demeter panicked, she sent Hermes to find the lost little girl. But when Hermes wove his way deep down into the underworld, he did not find a fearful and frail Persephone: he encountered the radiant, striking, powerful, and sexually rapacious Queen of the Underworld. She was just fine, thanks.

Still, she had to see her mom. Brow furrowed from the absurdity, she fretted her duty to Hades, worried that a trip to her chaste past might never end. The girls of the underworld wept crimson tears that they might never taste Persephone's sweet pussy again. Hades felt stretched by steel hooks inside. Taking his heart and his cock and his love in his hands, he cracked open a pomegranate and crushed the berries on Persephone's pillowy lips, staining them red forever. Then, she left.

She burned inside in the hollow spaces her lovers occupied, but her mother's name was still sweet on her tongue. Demeter, however, knew that the austere life she had fought to keep with her child was gone. The mother remembered a declaration that Zeus, King of the Gods had made from the heavens: for Persephone to return, she must be as pure as the day she left her mother's side. The garnet stain on Persephone's lips clearly showed that the girl had tasted the Fruit of Life. It could not be erased. And she liked it. Those tender lips curved into a soft, playfully hungry Mona Lisa smile, sweet with the surrender of innocence.

There's a lot of that sort of thing between these pages.

In the stunning, unbelievably arousing "Fly" by Valerie Alexander, it's night in Neverland and Tiger Lily is finally the sexually fierce young woman we always knew she'd become—much to the surprise of Peter and Wendy. "On Loan" by Lauren Wright describes a different sort of coming of age, where a woman is "lent out" by her husband to fulfill her number one fantasy of hotel room fuck-doll bliss, only to be surprised by a confrontation with a taboo that stems from her adolescent desires.

Trixie Fontaine takes us for a spin in the well-crafted "Fast Car, Not for Sale" where long roads and a girl's souped-up hot rod lead to one of the sweetest deflowerings a young man could dream up. "Waiting for the River" by Kris Adams brings us another flower aching to be plucked; here, a video camera gives a deeply shy young woman an excuse to open herself to another girl in a surprisingly exhibitionistic turn. The talented Xan West makes us feel "Lucky" in her tale of a submissive queer boi who surrenders to her mistress in every way, losing the virginity of complete sexual submission at a BDSM play party to a group of dominant strangers.

D. L. King's "Snug Designs" might just make you want to slip into something skin tight to read the rest of the book, in response to the protagonist's heated sexual adventures coming out as a rubber fetishist at the hands of a handsome fetish designer. "Courting Him" by Deborah Castellano is a decadent and delirious visit to the Victorian era where a fainting flower gets the upper hand of desire with her older male guardian and sinks into her first sexual takedown. In Janne

Lewis's "The Bitch in His Head" we see a takedown of great magnitude when a vicious germaphobic executive has the tables turned on him by his young sex partner, bringing us yet another sexual first for both characters.

When a woman meets a stern, bookish yet handsome antique store owner in Donna George Storey's "The Secret History of Lust," her desire to gain access to his members' only backroom collection has her opening herself up in ways she'd only imagined in order to pass his tests. In "Live Bed Show" by Elizabeth Coldwell, a young woman shocks herself by staging her own public sex deflowering in an Amsterdam store window. As is often the case with anal sex, the first time is the worst time; such is the case with the woman in Ms. Naughty's "Pasta with Blue Cheese and Anal" who finds that if at first you don't succeed, you can just have another "first" and enjoy ongoing success of the most blissful kind.

The myth of the first man and the first woman and the first penetration gets a biting turn in Alana Noël Voth's intense, powerful and lyrical "Eve." Jealousy turns quickly into curiosity—and then to overpowering sexual desire—in "What If?" by Cheyenne Blue, where a femme follows through with a scary-yet-hot voyeuristic fantasy of watching her butch lover perform a lesbian de-virginizing on a nervous but wanton straight girl. Scarlett French delivers a perfect tale of an experienced sex toy shop clerk who anxiously tries out her first mix of pain and pleasure with some very inspiring results, in "Good Pony." And for all those who have ever wanted to cross the line between teacher and student, don't miss the unconventional and very explicit upending of this iconic fantasy in Elisa Garcia's "Cardio."

Some things you try once and just hit a sweet spot so good

you have to make it a tradition, as with the creative gender-bending couple in Vanessa Vaughn's aptly titled "Switch." Lux Zakari's female protagonist wants to know just what's so hot about sex with girls, and when she asks her lover to "Describe It" she gets her first real view from between her own legs. Women who like sex with strangers love the endless line of first times stretching into their future: the eloquent and unerringly dirty "Decorations" by Sommer Marsden capitalizes on that notion with a couple whose public adventures in female submission describe a realm of fantasy I hadn't yet seen.

In Jacqueline Applebee's superb "Hush," silence is more than golden, it's a relentless aphrodisiac for one woman who initiates a man into her intricate world of silent pleasures. The supremely talented Janine Ashbless brings two archaeologists together in a tight squeeze for a first encounter of the desperately lusty kind, mimicking a sacred initiation in "Ritual Space." And upon deciding that enough is enough with her attraction to the boy next door, Kay Jaybee's "The Girl Next Door" surprises herself (and the boy) by taking the upper hand to create an unforgettably intense first for both of them, including at least one scene with a boy bent over a bathtub and a girl who fully comes into her own—and to sexual fruition—when she takes what she wants, rather than waiting around for it.

This collection is a ruby red pomegranate, sacred to Persephone. This anthology is a fragrant narcissus that opens the earth when picked. These stories are packed with first times, sexual initiations, women and men and genderqueers who try their number one desires on for the very first time—and like it, thank you very much. Virginity of all kinds—except the typical—is lost to the strains of shaking, thundering orgasmic bliss. There are furtive blowjobs, tense cunnilingus encounters, shockingly pleasurable spankings, desperate trysts, devious bindings, romantic couplings, and many, many taboos broken wide open like the path to the underworld itself. The strong women between these pages delight themselves, knowing that there's always another first time.

Of all the *Best Women's Erotica* volumes to date, this is the most unforgettable collection yet, a collection of delicious firsts, to be visited as often as Persephone beckons. I hope you like it as much as I do.

Violet Blue
San Francisco

FLY

Valerie Alexander

It's night on Neverland. The Lost Boys sit around the fire. Their war-painted faces glow with the fervor of boyhood delusion. They want adventure; their throats ache with unsung cries of battle and bloodlust. But the night won't begin until Peter arrives. Restless and agitated, the boys open beers and throw sticks into the fire and wait for him to return from his latest girl, his latest flight.

Across the island Tiger Lily also dreams of Peter. Naked on her bed, she toys with her tight amber tits, one fingertip circling her nipples. The other hand surfs down the silky dip of her navel until she cradles her own pussy under the pretence of someone else's touch. She is beautiful but she is ignored. Her clit hardens to the dream of something ambiguous, fantasies of a pointy-faced boy who at eighteen is all swagger and brashness. A boy whose thick golden-red hair is always askew, whose clever eyes are always alive with the possibility of danger. He is lithe and he is pretty, and from spying on him in the lake, she knows he is well endowed. But it's not his cock that haunts her dreams, it is his smile. He's a beautiful boy with a beautiful smile. All the girls want Peter.

Tiger Lily wants to fuck him more than life itself, but she wants more than that; she wants to pin him down and rub her pussy all over his face until he surrenders completely, until his endless taunts and stories are silenced. She wants to break his will and slap his face, wants to subsume his bragging in her sexual heat. Yet mostly what she wants is for Peter to teach her to fly. But he won't. Girls don't fly in Peter's world, not unless it's by holding on to him.

She rolls her clit between her fingers, slowly rubbing as she imagines that she is him. Now she's climbing rocks and scaling pirate ships, a prettier daredevil than he as she levitates with her long black hair flowing behind her like a flag. She knifes through the dark violet sky over Neverland until she sees Peter's last lover walking out of the lake. The girl is naked in the starlight and voluptuous as Peter likes his women to be. She's smiling dreamily as she towels off, perhaps lost in a reverie of that narrow-hipped boy who fucked her so soundly and never returned.

"I'll fuck you better than he ever will," Tiger Lily mutters and swoops down, still in her Peter guise, to push the girl down against the sand. Roughly she spreads her legs and fucks her with Peter's cock, pumping into her with savage thrusts.

"I knew you'd come back, Peter," the girl groans, arching her spine. "Oh, harder..."

But he never will come back, Tiger Lily thinks as her interest in the scene abruptly dies. She changes the fantasy to the last actual time she saw Peter, digging ammunition out of a pirate ship. Cheekbones smeared with dirt, bare-chested in ripped jeans, he talked excitedly of a fight he had won the previous night. She had been wearing her shortest dress, flexing her long bare legs for him. But he was too wrapped up in his story to even look at her.

But if he had. If he had turned and really seen her, the most hot-blooded girl on the island, he just might have knelt between her legs. Pushing her dress up her thighs, he would have pushed his thumb deep into her pussy, making her squirm there on the ship deck....

The thought sends a white bolt of heat ricocheting through her body, her cunt shuddering over and over around her fingers. Wetness soaks her hand, her thighs, as she furiously rubs herself into another flood of contractions. "I'm going to fuck you," Tiger Lily whispers, her legs spread wide for that phantom Peter thrusting into her. "I'm going to fuck you blind."

Collapsing back on her pillow, she licks the tangy, pearly strands of honey from each finger. Then she gets up and throws on her dress and heads off into the night.

The Lost Boys are still waiting to be found tonight by the boy they call their leader. Past the empty beer bottles and the boastful tales of girls fucked and discarded, their thoughts are anxious. They are not warriors or lovers, just followers still.

And then suddenly there he is at the fire with a self-satisfied smile. By the hand he holds his latest conquest: a hesitant-looking girl of about eighteen, softer than his usual girls and doe-eyed, her long brown hair wet and disheveled. She has the dazed and startled look of someone who has flown for the first time.

He pushes her forward for their appraisal. "This is Wendy."

Her wet cotton nightgown sticks to her body. It clings to her legs, is plastered to the hollow of her navel and sucked into the indentation of her belly button. But it's the outline of her nipples, stiff, with large aureole that are unexpected on such a petite young girl, that makes every boy there go hard. From the look in her eyes, they know she's too stunned by the flight to realize this. From Peter's lascivious grin, they know he flew her through a rainfall on purpose.

"Say hi," he urges, dropping his hand to gently cup her ass.

She blushes deeply. "Um…hello."

No one says a word. The boys stare at her with a grim and begrudging lust. Then Peter flashes a cocky smile at his tribe and says, "Be back soon," and leads Wendy away into the night.

Concealed behind her rock, Tiger Lily watches, scarcely daring to breathe as Peter saunters confidently to a banyan tree and tugs Wendy next to him. "Sorry I got you wet," he murmurs and kisses her ear, but not before another smug and secret grin escapes him at his own wordplay. Wendy doesn't notice it but only because she's growing suspicious now; she's looking uncertain of this long-limbed devil who shimmied up her drainpipe and crept through her bedroom window. That had to be how he did it, Tiger Lily thinks, his naughty grin appearing at the window like every repressed fantasy of her good girl imagination. For Wendy is definitely a good girl, procured by him in some hushed fancy place full of manicured gardens and teatime and other things Tiger Lily doesn't understand; that's Peter's secret type. Well-bred and easily awed and secretly burning to break out of the nursery. Instead the devil came to the nursery. Of course she let him in.

Wendy shivers now with some theatrics, prompting Peter to go predictable: "Are you cold? I'll warm you up."

So boring, so clichéd, Tiger Lily thinks, she should interrupt and teach them a thing or two. Still she wants to see Wendy's nightgown come off and that is exactly what happens, as Peter's mouth moves across her throat so skillfully that his hands push the nightgown up her hips without notice. Up it rises to reveal oval knees and soft pale legs. Something stirs deep in Tiger Lily's body. Moments later, Wendy's cunt comes into view, a soft mound of hair that doesn't quite conceal her shy cleft. Then her hips, rather wide and narrowing up into her waist, and finally her tits, full and round and creamy with those pink saucerlike nipples. Perfect breasts, the kind Tiger Lily wants to feel bouncing against her own as the two of them fuck each other into oblivion.

She drags her gaze up to check Wendy's face. The girl is scarlet with embarrassment and trembling. She should be spanked, Tiger Lily thinks, turned over my knee and spanked until her creamy ass is as red as her face. Then she'll cry and I'll lick her tears away....

Wendy's body is so pale and soft. This is a naked body that has never seen sunlight, Tiger Lily can tell, and this is a girl who has never felt a man's touch anywhere beneath the neck. That's clear as Peter, too fascinated to bother with sexual amenities now, traces one finger over her slit. Wendy's legs open and her eyes close with shame. "Oh, my god," she whispers.

Tiger Lily's blood grows hot. She cannot bear to watch

this a moment longer, Peter with yet another girl, so soft and obedient. In moments he will be playing with her clit and stroking the insides of her pussy until what will possibly be the girl's first orgasm slams through her—and then those soft doe eyes will gaze at him in a way no girl has ever gazed at her....

She scrambles silently through the trees, scales one and launches into her best pirate voice. The warning she calls out is ridiculous—Peter would be stupid to react to it so immediately, they both played pirate a dozen times together as kids, but his lust for war is stronger than his tactician's instincts and he abandons Wendy in a second. "Wait here!" he commands, all boy-man authority, and fairly skips off to the Lost Boys, his boys, who are already creeping toward battle.

Such an idiot, Tiger Lily thinks. Always forsaking the girl for the adventure, that's Peter. But no mind. She runs back through the trees and is at Wendy's side before the girl can put her nightgown back on.

Wendy is sure she is going to be murdered. The girl looming over her is like no girl she's ever seen, barely clad in a tiny buckskin dress, her long black hair alive in the night wind. Even her voice is different and commanding as she hisses, "Shut up! I'm Tiger Lily, I'm a friend of Peter's. The pirates are here, I'm going to rescue you." At the word *pirates,* something blank and primitive tightens Wendy's throat and she can't say a word as the girl snatches down the nightgown from its branch and ties the sleeve quickly and expertly in a gag through her pretty mouth. Wendy chokes a bit but she has been gagged before in her brothers' games and perhaps that is why she doesn't protest as the black-haired girl ties up her wrists with the other sleeve and leads her off into the forest.

Or perhaps she doesn't protest because of the cumulative shock of the night, which began with her tossing restlessly in her bed: too old at eighteen to spend her nights staring at the London rooftops through the nursery window. There was the shock of seeing a beautiful boy her own age appear at the window with a devilish smile, a boy who climbed in to shamelessly appraise her body through the skimpy nightgown before taking her hand and tugging her out the window. The shock of flying away over London, the shock of being stripped naked and spreading her legs as Peter touched her pussy. And now this, being tied up and led off into the woods, a naked captive. Not captured by a man like in her most forbidden fantasies but by a girl—a girl with hard lean muscles and long legs who moves so fast Wendy stumbles behind her.

Dazed as she is, it takes a minute to replay Tiger Lily's words and realize their basic contradiction: that if Tiger Lily is Peter's friend, why did she tie Wendy up? Her bare feet hurt from the sticks and debris of the jungle floor, and the night chill is making her stiff nipples ache. No one knows where she is. Yet soon enough they stop in a clearing, where Tiger Lily pushes her to her knees, before building a fire. She stockpiles a supply of kindling then takes her place opposite the flames.

Now the two girls stare at each other. Wendy can see every detail of her kidnapper's face in the firelight: a fiercely beautiful girl a little older than her with high cheekbones and fiery eyes, and a tough mouth that Wendy can tell will know exactly what to do to her. Everything about her wiry, taut body screams of sexual knowledge. This is a girl who knows what to do.

Then Tiger Lily drops her eyes and draws all that glorious black hair over one shoulder as she gazes into the fire. She seems absentminded, tracing a bruise on one bare thigh—and it is by following the movement of her hand that Wendy realizes Tiger Lily's legs are slightly open and her pussy is on full display. She seems either unaware of this or indifferent.

Wendy swallows nervously. She has never seen another woman's pussy, has never even gotten a good look at her own. She stares at it now, its mysterious pink folds, and wonders exactly where Peter had touched her to make that electric feeling ring through her.

Tiger Lily looks up, notices her gaze, and smirks. Wendy swallows again but doesn't shift her eyes. Yet Tiger Lily bounces abruptly to her feet, ending the show, and is at her side with that terrifying swiftness again. Roughly she pulls the knotted nightgown sleeve from her mouth. "Sorry."

Wendy's tongue, dry and stiff and tasting of cotton, moves tentatively around her mouth. Her knees hurt and Tiger Lily seems especially tall standing before her. "Who—why did you bring me here?"

"Why did Peter bring you to Neverland?" Tiger Lily is staring down at her with blank obsidian eyes, but Wendy can tell from the humming tension of her body that she is feeling far from blank at the moment.

"I—I don't know."

"He brought you here to fuck you, Wendy." Tiger Lily yanks the nightgown still tied around her hands and brings her roughly to her feet. Then she jerks Wendy's arms up over her head and moves her back and forth like a marionette, making her breasts bounce and sway.

Fear and arousal set off a throbbing between Wendy's legs. No one has ever taken such blatant control of her nor treated her so rudely, and it's exciting. As Tiger Lily pushes her back toward a tree, she finds herself turning up her face expectantly for the other girl's mouth. Instead Tiger Lily ropes the knotted nightgown on a branch, imprisoning Wendy's arms over her head. With a dirty smirk, she takes both her tits in her hands and begins to play with them.

"I bet you went to boarding school," Tiger Lily accuses.

"I did..."

"And I bet all you girls got in each other's beds at night."

"No! No, I mean, some girls, yes..."

"But not you?"

"No." Wendy shakes her head too fervently, her damp brown hair falling over her nipples. Tiger Lily impatiently flings the hair away, then slaps her breasts hard as punishment.

"You don't cover yourself around me." She pinches her right nipple, making Wendy gasp. "Understand?"

"Yes." That excitement in her pussy feels like melting honey now. Soon her thighs will be wet with it and Tiger Lily will see it and then she'll really be punished.

"So." Tiger Lily resumes feeling her tits, almost in a detached exploratory manner. "You never wanted a girl to do things to you."

"Well, I..." Wendy can't say the truth of this, which is that the shadow who tops her in her fantasies never has a face, let alone a gender. The shadow only has hands that stroke her, a tongue that licks her, a heat that's sometimes as hard as the hardest cock and other times pillowy as the softest breasts.

"Yes or no, Wendy. It's not that difficult a question."

"Leave her alone."

The rising heat cools in Wendy as she turns to see Peter in the clearing. He's here to rescue her, she realizes with a pang of annoyance, but she's not quite ready to be rescued. His mouth is set in a hard little line but those green eyes aren't quite as angry as his voice pretends. Yes, he's pissed that Tiger Lily stole his prey—his catch, Wendy thinks—but watching her tied up naked as Tiger Lily flicks at her nipples isn't something he's ready to stop just yet.

"You're the one who took her out of her own bed and flew her here, Peter," Tiger Lily taunts him. "Shouldn't you have left her alone?"

She smacks Wendy's breasts together a few times as if they're balloons, then dips her fingers between her legs. "Spread," she orders. Wendy's face burns hot now as she obeys, thighs shaking with anticipation of that first penetration of Tiger Lily's fingers. But Tiger Lily only traces one light finger around her clit in a soft, maddening circle without taking her eyes from Peter. *I am just a pawn to her,* Wendy thinks. The thought only makes her clit harder.

"Come on, Peter," Tiger Lily smiles. "Come rescue your pet."

So he's here at last. Peter looks as confused as Tiger Lily's ever seen him look, rubbing his hair in a way he does when he's thinking. It's rumpled around his face like a golden-red halo, as if he's an angel with a giant cock rather than the arrogant smartass she knows him to be. Once again he's shirtless, his bare chest smooth in the firelight, and two war stripes adorn his sculpted cheekbones. He stopped to paint himself to do battle with the pirates, how ridiculous. Tiger Lily gestures to the erection swelling in his pants.

"This is probably a little much for you so maybe you better just watch."

He flings himself at her with a roar. She dodges him well, with the practice of a hundred mock battles between them, then brings him down on his back. He looks stunned as she straddles him, quickly tying his hands tight with a piece of rope. But he recovers immediately.

"I can bust right out of these knots." He snarls at her in a way that reminds her of defensive animals trying to ward off a predator.

She shifts the heat and pressure of her pussy on his erection. He goes still. Subtly, with a clever smile, she rocks back and forth. His cock swells even bigger until a strangled groan escapes him.

Stupid boy, you don't know what you've been missing, she thinks. But all she says is: "I know what you want." Wendy's impatience and jealousy is palpable by the tree, but Tiger Lily ignores her for now. Staring into Peter's eyes, she opens her knees until she's showing him her pussy. So many times she's thought of Peter reaching for her, asking her, begging her, but now she's controlling him, and his submission is better than any of her dreams.

"Oh, fuck yeah," Peter mutters, his eyes locked on her.

With one quick move she swings up and settles her crotch directly on Peter's mouth. "Do it," she commands, not because he doesn't understand what she wants but because the sound of her own authority arouses her. She is soaked, wet from her clit to her asshole, and she takes pleasure in smearing it all over his nose and eyelids and cheekbones until his arrogant face shines with it.

"Fuck me," Peter moans against her, somewhat illogically as his tongue is desperately seeking her slit. She lifts herself just out of reach to tease him, then relents and sits down on him until the agile heat of his tongue squirms inside her.

Deep euphoria spreads through her. "Just like that," she whispers. She had known this would be good but just the sight of his face framed between her thighs sends an electric power through her body. Peter's endlessly talking tongue finally silenced and fucking deep in her pussy at last, his wrists tied so he can't fly. This is her moment.

Tiger Lily reverses direction on his face, leans over, and takes off his pants. Then the prize is in her hands at last: Peter's hard and straining cock. She rolls his shaft between her hands for only a moment before sucking it into her mouth, all of it, until her nose is buried in his balls. He tastes mustier than she expected, a boyish earthy taste, and his cock is as alive in her mouth as an animal. She pulls back to suck his head hard, tonguing it until he gasps.

Peter's not licking her pussy anymore; his tongue has slid up to frantically push inside her asshole, spearing her tightness over and over. And it's this that really does it for her: the knowledge of his tongue in her ass pushes her over into complete orgasmic mindlessness. Her pussy squeezes over and over as a hot gush of ejaculate floods out of her. Beneath her, he pulls back in surprise, but she sits down on his face and rides out her orgasm, grinding against his mouth until the last waves sputter out.

His hips bang the ground in frustration. "Tiger—"

She doesn't bother silencing him. Instead she returns to his cock, pressing it flat against his belly and wiggling her tongue up and down and around him before sucking him back inside her mouth. He writhes beneath her as if he's gone mad. "Don't—oh, god—don't stop." She keeps sucking him, feeling his balls tighten right up until the moment of no return—and then she does stop, because after making her wait for so many years, Peter really has no right to any kind of satisfaction this early in the night.

He sinks his teeth into the right cheek of her ass with a long, frustrated groan.

Oh, you bastard, she thinks with a mixture of indignation and amusement. She reaches back and feels the bite mark on her ass. Her fingers come away tinged with blood.

"You little bitch," she says and rings him across the face. It only turns him on more, making his hips dance. Her fingertip traces the bite again. Sometime tomorrow she will hold a mirror before her lifted legs and stare at the teeth marks as she fingers herself. But for now she feigns outrage.

"Get up." She yanks him to his feet, a naked and dazed boy looking almost sick with lust. His cock strains toward her as if magnetized. She shoves him against the tree and ropes him next to Wendy. Then she turns their bodies toward each other and begins to play with them like dolls. First she brushes Wendy's nipples against his chest until her face burns tomato red. Then she strokes Peter's cock over Wendy's slit, pressing his head hard against her clit until they both moan.

Tiger Lily laughs. "It's not going to be that easy."

She returns them to their separate positions and begins to toy with them. They look so beautiful, so flushed and horny. Sliding her fingers deep into Wendy's wet and swollen cunt, she rubs her in the way she likes herself, pressing her knuckles against the walls of her pussy. Wendy's pale body steams and shakes, she twists against her bonds and begs to be fucked.

Tiger Lily pulls out to stroke her clit. "Is this what you want?"

Wendy's legs strain open. "No...!"

"Tell me what you want."

"Just fuck me," Wendy gasps, a pink flush spreading across her breasts. She seeks to bring Tiger Lily closer by locking her ankles around her, but Tiger Lily deftly steps out of her way. "Don't stop, oh, please don't."

She fingers Wendy's clit for a few moments longer, then slides in three fingers, deep as she can go. Now she fucks her hard and rapidly, holding Wendy around the waist so she has to take it. The girl's cunt feels impossibly full and wet around her fingers and as a low growl breaks from her mouth, Tiger Lily feels her come; Wendy's velvety heat clenches her over and over until wet aftershocks tremble deep in her own pussy.

Tiger Lily gently withdraws her fingers and smears the glistening juices over Peter's parted lips. His eyes are locked on her, not Wendy, with reverence. *Oh, Peter,* she thinks, *we haven't even started.*

"Kiss me," she says. Her mouth, her tough mouth that has insulted and mocked him so many nights and cried his name alone in her bedroom, covers his. He tastes of Wendy's honeyed brine and then his own surprising sweetness. A sweet boy with a hard cock, captured at last. He's not flying anywhere until she's done with him, and the night has only begun as she presses her cool long body against his flushed and trembling one. Tiger Lily twists her arms up around his neck like a lover, like she dreamed of when she was young and romantic and naïve. But now she grabs his thick soft hair in her fist and twists it, pulling his head back so she can bite his lips.

"Anything you want," he begs in a low voice. "But please, please..."

What I want, she thinks, is to fly. And then it's happening, his cock pushes into the initial tightness of her pussy, demanding and inexorable yet torturously slow. She hooks one leg around his waist and brings him in deeper inch by teasing inch, until the cool sac of his balls rests against her. Already she's beginning to throb as they start to thrust, his heat and his hardness driving her up and up into blinding wet bliss, and then they're really fucking, faster and faster until at last Tiger Lily is flying.

LIVE BED SHOW

Elizabeth Coldwell

I sat on the end of the bed, looking out into the rainy Amsterdam night. My bare legs were crossed at the ankles and the straps of my nightdress were sliding down my shoulders, threatening to let my breasts spill free. It was a look designed to entice passersby to slow down, stop, maybe even think about making a purchase. But unlike the girls in the windows of the red-light district, over in the old part of town, I wasn't selling myself. I was selling the bed beneath me. Or at least that's how it started.

I came to Amsterdam because I fell in love with Jamie. I stayed because I fell in love with the city.

Jamie was an employee of the London arm of a Dutch investment bank, and a breed I normally went out of my way to avoid. I hated brash City types, with their loud voices, overconfident manner, and constant bragging about the size of everything from their annual bonuses to their cocks. But while the other blokes in his party were trying to grope my bum or stare down my cleavage as I served their meal, he was quieter, politer—and more than passably cute. At the end of the evening, he contrived to slip me his mobile phone number on the back of his business card, telling me he'd like to see me again. Three weeks after our first date, he told me he'd been seconded to the bank's headquarters in Amsterdam for six months, then asked me to move over there with him. It was a stupidly impulsive reaction on his part—and an equally impulsive one on mine to agree. But I was so sure it would work out that I packed in my waitressing job and gave my landlord notice on the flat I rented.

And it did work out. The bank had a ground-floor apartment on the Prinsengracht canal, a few minutes' walk from Jamie's new office and near to the Jordaan, the warren of streets packed with artsy-crafty little shops and brown cafés that were a magnet for tourists. It was quiet and tastefully decorated, with everything a tired businessman would need to entertain himself at the end of a long day, including a wall-mounted plasma screen TV, top-of-the-range sound system, and a power shower more than big enough for Jamie and me to use together. With no need to contribute to anything but our food bills, I was as close as I would ever come to being a kept woman, and I used the time I had to my advantage, roaming the canals with my camera. I had been trying to make a career in photography, which was what I had studied at art college, and this seemed like the ideal opportunity to build up a portfolio of work. I took black-and-white shots of everything from the queue of tourists snaking ’round the block as they waited to get into Anne Frank’s house to a couple cycling hand in hand by the side of the canal, to one of the window girls taking a cigarette break, lounging against a wall in her trashy lingerie and thigh-boots.

My forays into the red-light area weren’t all to take photos, though. I had discovered that though most of the sex shops were full of tatty novelties for the tourist trade, there were a couple of places selling quality fetishwear and interesting toys. So I invested in a few items to keep things spicy when Jamie came home: Velcro cuffs we could use to fasten each other to the bed; a string of anal beads that gave him the most incredible climax as I slowly pulled them out of his arse; a waterproof vibrator he used on me as the shower’s steamy spray beat down on us both, until my knees were sagging and I clutched at the tiled walls as I came and came again. I had more and better sex with Jamie, in those months in Amsterdam, than I’d ever had with anyone else.

But it takes more than great sex to keep a relationship going and, as the end of Jamie’s secondment approached, it became increasingly apparent to both of us that what had begun so explosively was fizzling out just as fast. Underneath it all, we liked each other well enough, but we really didn’t have that much in common.

When the time came for Jamie to arrange our flights to Heathrow, I told him not to bother with mine. I wouldn’t be going back to London—at least, not yet, anyway. When he didn’t even try to talk me out of staying, I knew I was making the right decision.

The problem was that I needed to sort out somewhere to live and get myself a job. I found an apartment without too much difficulty, in a tenement building a couple of tram stops away from the city's zoo. It was a little dingy compared to the place I'd lived in with Jamie, and up three flights of stairs, but it was cheap, and my neighbors seemed pleasant enough. An art gallery in the Jordaan had taken several of my photographs, and had even sold a couple, which covered the deposit on my apartment and the first month's rent, but I needed to do more than sell the odd photograph if I wanted to eat on a regular basis. At home, I would have been able to walk into just about any restaurant you cared to name and land waitressing work, but here, where my grasp of the language didn't extend much beyond "please," "thank you," and "beer," it was not going to be that simple.

So when I saw the sign being placed on the door of the bed shop, it seemed like fate. I had noticed the shop every time I traveled past it on the tram late at night, lit up when everything else was shuttered and silent. Today I had chosen to walk into the city center, past the Rembrandt Museum, and as I waited to cross the road, the middle-aged shop manager was sticking the sign in place. Helpfully, it was written in both Dutch and English: MODEL WANTED. My curiosity piqued, I darted inside the shop and found the manager behind the counter.

"*Goed dag,*" I said, then switched back to English, the limit of my Dutch pleasantries already reached. "I saw the sign. You're looking for a model. Well—here I am."

He looked me up and down. I might have been short by Dutch standards, though you could say that of any woman under five feet ten, and I hoped that wouldn't count against me. It didn't.

"You've modeled before?" he asked.

"Well, to be honest, no. But I really need a job"

"Okay. This isn't exactly runway work, anyway. I'm looking for someone who can make the most of this"—and he gestured to the bed in the window display which, he told me, was on special promotion. As he described the job requirements, I couldn't believe what I was hearing. The model needed to arrive at the shop just before nine at night, change into her nightwear—in the staff toilet, not the window, he added hastily, as it wasn't that kind of establishment—putter around for an hour and then go to bed. The idea was to convince passersby the bed was so comfortable that you could get a decent eight hours' sleep even in such an artificial environment and thus nodding off at home would be a cinch. The money he was offering wasn't great, but it was enough. And I didn't need to be able to speak a single word of Dutch. It was perfect, and I told him so. I was hired. We shook hands on the agreement, and I went off to buy a new nightdress for my first public appearance.

I settled into the routine very quickly. Wim, the shop manager, would be waiting for me every night at about ten to nine. He would let me into the shop, we would exchange a few pleasantries, and then he'd go on his way. I would change into my nightdress and get into position on the bed. I had my iPod, onto which I had downloaded a *Teach Yourself Dutch* course, books and magazines to read, and an eye mask to block out the glare of the shop's fluorescent lighting.

It soon became obvious, however, that wasn't enough. I was managing to get a surprisingly good night's sleep, once the rumble of the trams on the road outside died down just after midnight, but the reading matter I had brought wasn't enough to keep me stimulated. And if there was one thing I needed since I'd split up from Jamie it was stimulation—mental and physical.

Not only that; I didn't feel as though I was doing enough to attract the attention of passersby. Oh, they would slow down a little as they walked past, take a quick look at the strange girl sitting in a shop window reading, but they very rarely stopped, and they almost never paid attention to the sign in the window highlighting the low cost and exceptional comfort of this king-sized bed. I needed to put on a performance.

The following night, I arrived with all the equipment needed to give myself a pedicure, and spent a long time massaging my feet with body lotion before meticulously applying a coat of red varnish to my toenails. This time, people did stop, did take notice and did, once they had tired of looking at my bare legs and the tops of my breasts where they peeped out above the lacy edging of my nightdress, look at the bed and, I guessed, wonder how it might fit in their own bedrooms. There were a couple of men who did nothing but stare at the arch of my instep and my delicate toes, but to each his own—and after all, I was the one in charge of this little display, they were the ones who stood on the outside, gazing hungrily in at their fetish made flesh.

The realization that I could tease and tempt, safe and inviolate behind glass, awakened in me an exhibitionistic streak I had never realized I possessed. Now, instead of huddling under the covers, ignoring my potential audience as I completed a sudoku puzzle, I perched on the end of the bed, showing off. Making them come to me. Making them want me.

I would wait till a likely-looking man approached and then I would casually, carelessly bend forward, giving him a view right down my nightdress to my breasts. Or I would cross my legs, flashing him a pair of knickers pulled up snugly against the contours of my pussy. After a couple of nights, I no longer bothered putting on the knickers. I wantonly let strangers see my pink lips, the little tuft of soft brown hair, and sent them away with a bulge in their pants that ached for relief.

It wasn't just the men who watched me, either. You'd be surprised how many of the women who passed seemed to be hoping for a glimpse of my tits. Perhaps it was just to compare them to their own, but I suspected that some of them looked because it turned them on.

Enjoying myself now, I began to fetch the vibrator I had bought to share with Jamie in to work. I will never forget the expression on the face of the first man who watched me run the buzzing toy first along the length of my arm, then slowly down my neck. His eyes bugged in disbelief as I played it over my breasts, causing my nipples to pucker into hardness. He hoped, as every man who followed him did, that I would take the vibrator down between my legs and let it press against my clit. I wanted to, desperately, but something always held me back from going all the way.

Only once I was back in my apartment did I give in to the need for release. I would lie back on my own bed, smaller and with a lumpier mattress than the one I had become used to in the shop, and masturbate, always with the same fantasy in my mind. I would imagine myself in the shop window, legs widely parted, thrusting the vibrator up into myself, and outside, some anonymous voyeur would be watching and wanking his hard cock till his spunk spattered against the glass. At that point I would always come, screaming out my pleasure in the quiet little apartment and already eager for the coming night.

I had no idea whether Wim was aware of what I actually got up to when he left me in his shop for the night, but he couldn't fail to notice the increased customers I had brought in. He told me that every day people would come and lie on the bed in the window. I imagined most of them were hoping for a sniff of my scent, trapped in the sheets, but more than a few of those who sampled the mattress went on to order a bed of their own.

One morning, as he paid me my wages, he told me he had some important news. He needed to take a few days off to look after his sick mother, and his nephew, Jaap, would be letting me into the shop in his absence. Apparently, Wim had no sons of his own, and so was training the lad to take over the business when he retired. I merely nodded, having been worried he was about to tell me the special promotion was over and he was terminating my employment.

When I saw Jaap, a small part of me hoped that Wim's mother's illness would be of the lingering variety. The man was gorgeous; in his early twenties, with a long, lean body; short, spiky blond hair and an open smile. I caught him giving me an appreciative glance or two as he let me into the shop, but I told myself not to make anything of it. It was just my hormones responding to the first man in a long time who'd admired my body without there being a pane of glass between us. Still, that night, as I knelt up on the bed and caressed my body, I imagined it was Jaap who was staring at me through the shop window, Jaap who was silently encouraging me to spread my legs and touch myself for him....

And as I sat on the end of the bed, looking out into the rainy Amsterdam night, I heard a noise behind me, and turned. Someone was in the shop! The figure stepped out from the shadows of the curtaining display, and I realized it was Jaap. But surely he'd locked up and left hours ago? I shook my head, trying to dismiss him as a figment of my overheated imagination, but as he walked over to the bed, I knew he was real.

"I know what you do," he said, coming to stand beside me. "My friend, Peter, saw you a couple of nights ago. He said you gave him a flash of that cute little pussy of yours. And I wanted to see for myself. That's why I volunteered to look after the shop for my uncle. That's why I came back tonight."

"But if you wanted to watch me through the window..." I began.

He shook his head. "No, I wanted the real thing. I want to touch it. Taste it."

His words set a pulse beating fiercely between my legs. I watched as he stripped out of his jeans and T-shirt and came to sit beside me on the bed, wearing only a pair of black briefs that held his cock coiled within them. He looked huge, and though I knew we shouldn't be doing this, I couldn't stop myself.

I flopped back, pushed my nightdress up around my hips, and slowly, deliberately opened my legs. His gaze was drawn like a magnet to the folds of my sex, already wet from all the teasing and stroking I'd given myself earlier. I couldn't see if there were any passersby staring through the window, but if there were, I knew their view would have been obscured by the bulk of Jaap's body. They could only imagine what might be happening, and envy the fact that what I had shown them only in glimpses, he was seeing in all its blossoming glory.

"Beautiful," he murmured, and traced a big finger along my lips. Desire had made me submissive, and I lay there, letting him explore everywhere from the tip of my clit to the pucker of my arsehole. I barely knew the man, and yet already I was letting him touch all my most intimate places. And when he replaced his finger with the firm point of his tongue, I almost squealed in delight.

I forgot I was in such a public place, forgot all about our potential audience as Jaap proceeded to lick me deliciously and thoroughly. Much as I had enjoyed fucking Jamie, he had always felt that oral sex was just a minor detour on the way to the final destination. For Jaap, however, this was clearly a most important part of the journey. My hips arched up toward his face, and my hands grabbed fistfuls of the bedsheets as his tongue probed and dallied, taking me all the way to the summit of my orgasm.

But just before he got there, he pulled his mouth away. I wanted to grab him by the hair and force him back into place, but he shook his head. He pressed his lips to mine, letting me taste myself. "Patience," he said. "It'll be all the sweeter when it happens."

As I waited, wondering where he had learned his incredible technique, he fished a condom from his jeans pocket. He casually discarded his briefs, and his cock emerged, big and beautifully in proportion to his six-foot frame. I definitely needed to be wet to take that, I thought, as he slid the condom down over its substantial length—but I was ready for him.

It was his turn to lie down now, as he urged me to get on top of him. I thought for a moment I saw a curious, mustachioed face peering in, but the rain was falling harder than ever, and it was hard to imagine that anyone might stand for long in that weather, even with a live sex show unveiling before their eyes.

A wicked thought struck me and I grabbed my eye mask, slipping it down over Jaap's head to blindfold him. He smiled, clearly turned on by such a simple but kinky trick, and let me take charge. I began to feed his cock into me, gradually lowering myself down. I felt myself stretching wide, and the sensation was glorious. I rose and fell on him, controlling the pace, controlling the pleasure. The springs creaked gently beneath us as a bed that had only ever been intended for display purposes was finally christened in the most erotic fashion.

His hands were on my breasts, pressing them together, and he was muttering something I didn't understand, though the meaning was clear enough. He was loving this moment, and so was I. I rode him harder, gripping his thick thighs with my knees, and when I reached a finger down to play with my own clit, my pleasure peaked unstoppably. I was still feeling the spasms gripping me when Jaap groaned and let out what I assumed to be some choice Dutch swear words as he came.

We slumped together for a moment, and when we pulled apart I almost expected to see someone standing on the pavement outside, applauding. But the street was empty, and if we'd had an audience, it had already disappeared.

That was my last night in the window. Crossing the line is fun, but you can only do it once. I asked Jaap to tell his uncle when he returned that I had been offered a job elsewhere. It was a lie, obviously, but a week later an opportunity arose to become a tour guide for English-speaking parties in one of the museums, and I took it. I went past the bed shop on my way back from work—or Jaap's apartment, because even if we couldn't have sex in public, that didn't mean we couldn't keep doing it in private—but I never saw another girl doing Wim's special promotion work. And I always wondered whether anyone bought the display bed, and whether they ever had as much fun on it as I did.

WHAT IF?

Cheyenne Blue

"What if I wanted to visit Paris?" Peta began. "Would you come with me?"

Our favorite game. I rolled over and rested my head on my folded arms. Peta was also on her stomach, chewing on a grass stalk, the sunlight gilding her hair to a soft gold.

"Depends," I said. "Would we fly or sail?"

"Sail," she replied without hesitation. "On an oceangoing yacht, just you and me, and a discreet crew to actually make the thing go. Champagne and sunsets at sea—"

"Motion sickness and stinky pump toilets—"

"Waves lapping on the hull, dolphins leaping at the prow."

"I don't think there are dolphins in the Atlantic," I said, "but okay so far. Where would we stay when we got to Paris?"

"In a garret in the artists' quarter. Up seven flights of creaky wooden stairs. We'd have baguettes with unsalted butter and cherry jam for breakfast, and strong, thick coffee, and we'd wander the boulevards hand in hand buying cheese."

"Would this garret have hot water?"

"Sometimes. Other times it would be clanking pipes and a tepid dribble."

"Not so keen on that," I said. "So who would do the cooking?"

"Moi!" Peta showed one of her few French words.

I rolled onto my side and let my hand trace her sinewy arm. She looked damn hot in the white singlet, her tanned biceps displayed to perfection, and a hint of brown nipple showing through the clinging white top. "You win," I said. "I'll come with you."

She grinned and rolled onto her back, her arm over her eyes to keep out the sun. "So I get another go?"

"Yup. That's the game."

"What if..." And she hesitated.

"Can't think of anything?" I teased.

"What if I wanted to sleep with Suzie? Would you let me?"

My fingers stilled on her biceps. The muscle was taut—too tight—underneath my hand. The moment was frozen in time. Distantly, I registered traffic noise out on I-25, the way the sun skidded off the peaks of the Rockies turning the white snowcaps to amber, the bug that marched purposefully over Peta's hip. The tickle of the short grass of Washington Park, already turning brown even though it was only May.

She was watching me, her eyes intent on my face, the time measured in the slow deep breaths that separated one plane of my life from the next.

Normal. Act normal.

"Just one time, or for a long time?"

"Just one time. Suzie's straight. Once would be enough."

Self-proclaimed straight, but 100 percent bi-curious. She came into the Pink Light on Colfax most weekends, sitting up at the bar all quivering eagerness, shooting pool haphazardly, flirting with the butches, but always pulling away at the last moment, when it was time to leave, time to go home, time to go fuck.

"Would you take her to a motel, or go back to her place?"

"I'd take her to our apartment," Peta said.

Our apartment. Our Washington Park den, all polished floors and wide windows that let the setting sunlight stream through over the tops of the Rockies, over our collection of houseplants, over Moggie, our cat, as she lay sunning herself on the sill. Over our lives. Into our lives.

I glanced at Peta; she was still watching me and the slight quiver of her hard brown abs below the crop top told me how deadly serious she was.

Continue the game, continue the pretence.

"What would you do with her?"

"I'd kiss her in the shadows between the pools of light on Colfax, and she'd sigh into my mouth in acceptance. She's wanted this; she's wanted someone to seduce her slowly. It's all too hard and fast for her in the Pink Light. Then, I'd take her hand and we'd go home."

"How would you get home?"

"Taxi. You and I never take the car when we go to the Pink Light as we always drink too much to drive. And Suzie would have had a couple too many, deliberately for Dutch courage. She wants to go through with this, she's just afraid of the unknown."

"Us? Where am I then?"

"You're following me and Suzie down Colfax, a few paces behind, and you're watching. Watching how our hands intertwine, watching the slant of her hips toward me, watching how she skips and prances like a little girl being led home by Daddy. And then you're in the front seat of the taxi, trying hard not to look at what we're doing in the back."

"What are you doing in the back?"

"Gentling her. Soothing her skitteriness, like she's a filly that needs breaking. Calming her nerves, as now she knows there's no going back. So I'm holding her curved against my side, and I'm stroking that wispy blonde hair back from her face. Telling her how pretty she is, how desirable. Maybe I'm kissing her cheek, soft little kisses, sliding around to the edge of her lips."

"Why our apartment?"

Peta sat up in one smooth movement and her hand came out to touch me. The first time, I noted absently, that she'd touched me since this game began. Only it wasn't a game anymore. Her fingers walked down my arm and laced themselves with mine.

"If it's in our apartment I'm not excluding you. You're a part of it, Ria. How could it happen otherwise?"

It need not happen at all, I wanted to shout. She could forget this crazy idea, this macho strutting to take Suzie's lesbian virginity. Was it something to boast about in the Pink Light? I wasn't sure I could handle that, if it was; sitting there, stony-faced, staring into my beer, pretending not to care as Peta told and retold the story of her conquest.

And what of Suzie herself? Would she fade into the woodwork after this, curiosity assuaged? Or would she hang around, wanting more? Would she want Peta for her own?

I stared down at our intertwined fingers, at Peta's hard blunt paws, at my plump white manicured fingers. I didn't know what to say.

A thump in the small of my back toppled me forward, my head coming to rest on Peta's knee. She settled me carefully, stroking the hair from my eyes with one hand, while the other scooted the football, which had hit me, back to its owner, reassuring them that there was no damage, no apology necessary.

Her expectant face peered down at me. "You okay?"

Somehow, I thought she meant more than simply the blow from the football. "I think so."

She nodded, and a finger traced the outline of my lips. I kissed it as it went by.

"So what happens when we arrive at our apartment?" I asked.

"Despite my consideration in not jumping her in the cab, Suzie's still nervous, so she asks if she can have a drink. I'm putting on some music—something mellow, like k.d. lang—so you go and get a bottle of red. You can't find the corkscrew—no doubt I've put it away in the wrong drawer again—so when you return, Suzie and I are dancing.

"I'm holding her close, and my hips are pressed into hers. My hand's on her butt, molding her close to me."

"Are you packing?"

Her hand shifted to my arm, and her thumb stroked the side of my breast. I turned to rub my cheek against her thigh. She wasn't packing now.

"Yes, so Suzie can feel the outline of my rigid cock. She sighs a little and slides her arms around my waist. That's the sign I've been waiting for. Now I can move into a higher gear, so I kiss her properly. Harder, deeper, really tasting her.

She kisses me back, her tongue tangling with mine.

"You can see we don't need the wine now, so you put it down, and sit on the couch."

"Does Suzie mind that I'm there?"

"She never speaks to you, as if by doing that, she'd have to acknowledge that you were there, watching. She's pretending that it's just me and her."

"And what about you?"

"I'm happy you're there. I wouldn't be doing it unless you were. I want you to get off on this as much as me, so I'm putting on a show for you. Suzie's wearing a skirt of some soft cotton. And, slowly, inch by inch, I'm gathering it up at her butt. Now you can see the backs of her thighs. Now, the edge of her panties. What do they look like, Ria?"

"Peach," I said, without hesitation. "A real girly-soft peach. And lacy. She's worn her sexiest underwear deliberately. It looks good against her pale skin."

Peta's thumb stroked soft circles, inching ever closer to my nipple with each pass. I sighed gently—as Suzie would do—in acceptance of the spell her words were weaving.

"And her legs," prompted Peta. "What do they look like?"

"Pale. She keeps her skin out of the sun. Only a hint of color. Soft legs. She's not the sporty type. She stays slim by picking at her food, not by exercise."

"When I get her skirt up to her waist," Peta continued, "I slide my hand down the top of her panties. Her butt is smooth and warm, and I can feel her shiver. I curve my hand down until I'm tickling the crease between ass and thigh; nearly, but not quite touching the fine hairs of her cunt. We're still moving slowly to k.d. lang, and I turn us around so that you have a full view of her ass—"

"And that's when you slip your fingers lower, farther around, and move one up into her pussy. She gives a little gasp of surprise—she didn't expect you to move so quickly—but now it's too late, and you've got one, now two, fingers pistoning in and out of her cunt. She's wet; I can hear the squishy sound your fingers make—"

"She's not doing anything to me; she's simply holding on to my waist and riding my fingers. I want to add more, but the angle's all wrong. She hasn't touched me at all; my nipples are hard and tender against my shirt, and I want to adjust my cock so that the base of it gives me friction, but I don't want to let go of her. But, it's enough; as you're watching me, watching us, and your eyes are avid and intent, and now you're undoing the button on your jeans. You're shy; you don't want Suzie to see you, but I can see everything. You're wearing—"

"Simple black cotton panties. Unlike Suzie, I didn't dress for the occasion. They're old, and the waistband is a little loose, so I can work my fingers down to my pussy without pushing my jeans down farther. My thighs are straining the denim apart, but it's enough. I've got a finger on my clit. You can't see my pussy, but you know what I'm doing, you know how I like to touch myself."

My eyes were closed to the rhythm of our words. Peta's thighs were hot underneath my cheek, and her own musky scent filled my nose, blending with the tang of grass clippings. I knew—I hadn't forgotten—that we were in one of Denver's busiest parks, but it was mattering less and less. I wanted to turn my face into her pussy, pull down her shorts, spread her thighs, and push my nose into her thatch, my tongue into the folds and crevices of her cunt, and suck and slurp and drown in her juices. But even in the words she was weaving, Peta knew me well; public sex just wasn't my thing. I pressed my thighs tightly together so that the pressure grew, and continued.

"I know you want to fuck her, but there's no way to move into the bedroom without breaking the spell. So—"

"I decide to take her here, on the floor, on the only rug in the whole apartment, in front of the wide window that overlooks downtown. So, slowly, I withdraw my fingers from her cunt. She mews a little in disappointment, but she's looking at me with wide eyes, waiting to see what happens next. Her cheeks are flushed, the pinkness creeps down the front of her T-shirt. She still hasn't touched me, she won't touch me, that's too much for her right now. But it doesn't matter. I'll get my own pleasure, and your eyes watching me all the way will bring me there.

"I step back from her, and yank my T-shirt over my head, kick off my sandals, and push my shorts and jocks down, so that I'm naked in front of her. She may not want to touch me yet, but I want there to be no mistake as to whom she is fucking. My cock springs free, hard and needy. Her hands rise, and her fingers flutter in front of my breasts. She's wanting to touch, but hasn't the confidence. It's irking me a little; she's all take and no give, this woman. So I curve a hand behind her head and press her head to my breast. Her nose bumps my nipple, she gasps, and hesitates, but now my nipple is at her lips, and she opens her mouth, sucks me in, tongues me, then suckles harder.

"Your eyes meet mine, over her head, and I wonder what you're thinking, seeing another woman touch me, suckle me, the first in our five years together."

"Part of me wants to scream and drag her off you, kick her perfect little pink bi-curious butt out of our apartment, but most of me wants to see you fuck her, make her scream and shudder around your cock. And now, I'm touching my own nipple under my top, flicking it in time to her suckling. But she's still dressed. I want to see more than her panties. Get her naked. Now!"

"Yes, ma'am! I push her away from me, and shuck the skirt off her like the husk off an ear of corn. She stands passively, raising her arms to let me pull her shirt over her head. Her bra matches her panties—she definitely dressed with this in mind. But I don't stop to admire them; I hook my fingers in the waistband and pull hard.

"She gives a little strangled cry; the panties must be digging into her sensitive pussy before the material gives way, but I don't stop, and there's a loud rip. I toss her ruined panties to one side, and she's naked, looking up at me with pleading in her eyes. I hesitate; I know she wants me to kiss her, but it's you I'm thinking of. A kiss at this moment is such an intimate act, I don't know if you want me to kiss her."

"Kiss her," I order. My eyes are still closed, but Washington Park has faded to a distant background buzz. It's just me, Peta, and the ethereal Suzie, in the living room of our apartment.

"So I kiss her and she responds with gratitude. She wants the romance as well as the sex. She tastes of bourbon, so different from you. But kisses aren't enough—"

"Fuck her. Take her now."

"I direct her hand to my cock. She's now so far gone that she grasps it eagerly, stroking up and down the shaft. I push my hand on her shoulder, and she sinks to the floor underneath my touch. I kneel over her, part her soft white thighs with one hand. She's wet; I can see her pussy lips shining. Her pussy hair is so blonde and fine that at first I think she's shaved herself. She has sparse, soft hair, like a young girl."

"Do you go down on her?"

"I think about it, but I can see you, and your fingers working away underneath your panties. Your face is red, and your breath is hitching in your throat. I know you're about to come, and I want to see that. So no, I don't. I kneel between her thighs—"

"Which way are you facing? Can she see me?"

"I'm looking directly at you, over her head. If she turned her head to one side she could see you, but she doesn't. Her gaze is fixed on me, looming over her, cock in hand."

"And then—"

"I fuck her."

Oh, god. Wash Park was gone, gone, gone, and my entire being was focused on our apartment and what we were doing—would do? may do?—there.

"I enter her with one sure thrust," continued Peta, "and she clutches my shoulder and pants into my face. Her other hand reaches around, underneath her thigh to feel my cock and how it fits inside her. I start to move, and every thrust rubs my cock on my clit. It won't take much until I come.

"I rise up and reach between our bodies, find her clit, and rub. And she comes. Just like that, clenching down on my cock, shuddering underneath me, her pretty white teeth biting her bottom lip. Her body goes limp; she lies as flaccid as a wet towel. She's not a giving lover, but I don't care. My eyes meet yours over her head—"

"You thrust harder, faster, until her whole body is shaking with the force of it. It must be uncomfortable for her—your cock is thick and long—and the force of your pounding must be hurting her, but you don't stop. Because you're about to come—"

"And your fingers are working frantically, and your face is flushed and your hair is wet with sweat. Any moment now—"

"I come. It's a long, hard, shuddering climax, my body jackknifes double, and my thighs are rigid. And I scream, uncaring of Suzie, great gulps of air, forcibly exhaled—"

"I'm coming with you. My final thrusts are almost savage, but I'm coming hard, deep into Suzie. She whimpers underneath me. I stroke her hair gently from her brow, soothing her with incoherent murmurs, but my eyes are still hooked on you, and how beautiful you look in the low light, your sweaty hair over your face. And now it's over, doubt sets in. My eyes plead with you for reassurance—"

"I smile. It's okay. Suzie lies forgotten underneath you, and you and I communicate with our eyes. I love you."

"I love you, too."

I opened my eyes, back in the real world, Washington Park swimming back into focus. Peta loomed above me, her hand knotted in the fabric of my T-shirt, taut with the spell of our words. She kissed me, her tongue running in demand around my mouth. I could smell her excitement in the cradle of her thighs, the waves of musk that permeated her shorts.

"So," she said, when she lifted her head. "Shall we do it?"

My cunt throbbed. "Do what?"

"Paris. You said you'd come with me. We might need to fly instead of taking the yacht, but we could still rent a garret and make love to the sound of the Parisian traffic."

Right then, I'd have followed her anywhere. "Let's do it!"

THE BITCH IN HIS HEAD

Janne Lewis

I arrived an hour ago at the London flat that Dimitri's company keeps for business guests. I have unpacked my suitcase and changed into the light blue silk and lace teddy Dimitri bought for me in Paris. I am wandering around the bedroom holding a bouquet of butt plugs in assorted sizes and a tube of lubricant trying to decide where I can hide them.

The phone rings.

Corbin, Dimitri's assistant, wants to know if the flat has been arranged to suit his boss's needs.

"I think everything is okay." I scan the room. Dimitri has a long list of domestic requirements. "The flat looks immaculate, the bed linens look fine." I lift the neatly tucked corners of the expensive Frette linens. "The plastic cover on the mattress is in place."

Dimitri cannot sleep on a mattress on which others have slept unless it is swathed in a protective layer of plastic.

"The duvet looks new and appropriately silky." I open the closet. "Silk dressing gown, silk pajama bottoms. I think you've covered all the fabric bases."

There are many fabrics and textures Dimitri cannot abide; chief among these are wool, polyester, and latex. His position with a multinational pharmaceutical company requires him to wear latex gloves. He manages to do this for brief periods but the thought of putting on a latex condom makes him nauseated.

"I brought new glasses and his favorite whiskey," Corbin tells me. "There's some champagne in the fridge for you, ducks, if you survive your night with Mr. Hyde."

"Is he that bad?"

Corbin lowers his voice.

"He's vile. He made two senior sales managers cry this morning and then tried to sink his fangs into me. I told him that if he wasn't nice to me, your flat would not be priss perfect which would probably make him impotent, or he'd have to fuck you in his own flat, in which case it would no longer be his sterile haven." Corbin snorts. "He turned purple and left me alone. His need for your pussy is my employment protection plan."

"Charming."

"Sorry, ducks, but it's true. Work your magic, and send him back to us nice and lamblike."

I laugh.

"I'll do my best, Corbin."

Poor Dimitri. The Bitch in His Head has been riding him hard.

The Bitch in His Head is my secret name for Dimitri's mix of neurotic tendencies and obsessive-compulsive disorder. The Bitch isn't a nasty dominatrix in leather boots and corset; She is too suave for that get up, too elegant. She is beautiful and cruel like the queen in Sleeping Beauty or the evil White Witch in the Narnia stories. She is my enemy, but I know without Her in control, the brilliant, sophisticated, charming Dimitri would never have settled for someone as ordinary as me. Still, there are many times when I wish the Bitch would take a long vacation from our ménage à trois and leave Dimitri and me alone.

I put the handset down. It rings again.

"Yes, ducks?" I say, thinking it is Corbin calling back.

"Don't use that inane phrase, Alexa." Dimitri's deep voice betrays his irritation. "You sound like a fool."

My pulse instantly quickens when I hear his voice.

"Hello, Dimitri. Lovely to hear from you. Did you get my latest test results?"

Blood samples and oral and vaginal swabs are now part of my weekly routine. The Bitch in His Head would not let Dimitri near me without them.

"Yes."

"Are we off to the races?"

"I need you, Alexa," he says. His voice cracks. He is obviously not in the mood for jokes. "It's been three shit-filled weeks. I need you so badly."

"I know. Corbin told me you've been rather unpleasant."

"Corbin is an idiot. This office is full of idiots. I hate every stinking inch of this city and everyone in it. The only place I want to be is in bed with you and deep in your cunt."

Heat floods my body. My nipples harden. I want him as much as he wants me.

"That's why I'm here, love."

I hear him sigh.

"I'll be there in ten minutes. I'm rock hard. Be ready for me."

The Bitch in His Head does not let Dimitri masturbate himself to orgasm. She keeps him agonizingly frustrated. Usually Dimitri is a sensitive, gentle, generous lover. When we've been apart for a while and She's been torturing him, he will grab me and throw me on my back and bend me into a ball so my knees are by my ears, and he'll fuck me so hard I'll have to use deep breaths like a woman in labor to withstand his onslaught. He'll pound me over and over until I'm praying for him to come. Finally, when tears have started to leak from my eyes, he will roar and tremble and shoot his wad into me. After, he will wrap his arms around me and tell me how grateful he is to me, how much he depends on my understanding, how much he loves me.

I can't help thinking that this kind of fucking is mostly about the Bitch in His Head and has little to do with me. Maybe the Bitch is whispering in his ear, urging him on. Maybe Dimitri is trying to fuck the Bitch into silence. I have thought long and hard about how to avoid that situation this weekend. That is where my bouquet of butt plugs comes in.

I push the butt plugs and the lubricant under the pillow on the right side of the bed. It is not the most ingenious hiding place, but I'll risk it. I put the handcuffs and the coils of silk rope under the duvet.

I lie on the bed with my head on the pillow disguising the lumps I've left. The sheets feel cool and smooth on my bare skin. I raise my wrist and smell the delicate scent of violets, a scent Dimitri has specially made for me. I am not sure if it is the fragrance or the change Dimitri and the Bitch have made in my wardrobe but in the year and a half I've been fucking Dimitri, I've had more propositions from men and women than in my previous thirty-four years combined.

I run my hands over the silk teddy and feel the heavy weight of my breasts in my hands and squeeze them. Dimitri told me it was the combination of my large breasts and serious expression that attracted him to me the night we met at a party. When he found out that I was a tax lawyer—careful, methodical, trained to give meticulous attention to detail—he decided to risk asking me out, hoping that one day, he'd be able to explain himself to me.

I run my fingers down the silk on my belly to where the teddy's lace hem rises over the bush of my pubic hair. The insides of my thighs and the skin on my legs are freshly waxed and silky smooth. I splay my legs open and stroke the soft insides of my thighs, just grazing the tender folds of my labia. When I fly home to New Jersey, I'll have purple marks on my thighs from Dimitri's hands.

I hear the flat door open and slam shut.

The sound makes my heart race, but I don't move from the bed. I close my eyes and gently stroke the edges of my labia. The inside of my cunt passage spasms. I press one finger down the center of my cunt and feel my heat and moisture. I think about Dimitri's muscular tongue, his thick cock, the tight anus he has not yet allowed me to explore. I let the tip of my finger enter my cunt. I am slick inside. I groan with longing.

"You'd better be thinking of fucking me while you're doing that."

I open my eyes, turn my head, and see Dimitri standing in the bedroom doorway.

He is such a beautiful man.

He has taken off his jacket and is unknotting the silk tie around his neck. His green eyes flick over the room. The arches of his black eyebrows are perfect counterpoints to the high curves of his cheekbones. His black hair is thinning, but his mustache is a thick black bristle, like a neon sign proclaiming his virility.

I am still stroking myself with one hand. I take my other hand to my breast and pull the top of the teddy down so one of my nipples is exposed. I rub my nipple, and stretch it slightly, waiting for the Bitch in His Head to be satisfied with the room and let Dimitri look at me.

Dimitri unbuttons his shirt, his eyes still moving around the room. I wonder what the Bitch is looking for.

"Actually," I say, my voice a low purr, "I was thinking about this guy on the plane."

Dimitri drapes his shirt on a chair. He walks to the foot of the bed, and reaches for his belt. I love his broad chest with its pale skin and pink nipples and curly black hair.

"What guy?" His lips hardly move under his mustache, but his green eyes are now fixed on me.

"The guy sitting next to me. He looked at me like he was a cat and I was the proverbial bowl of cream."

I hear the *ssh* of the leather as Dimitri slides the belt out of his pants.

"He said he would love to show me around London. Told me he would make it well worth my while to change my plans." I laugh. The guy was not bad looking and before I had Dimitri, I would have been thrilled with his attention.

Dimitri holds his belt in one hand and scowls at me. I can well imagine him reducing his employees to tears.

"Did he touch you?"

I don't know if it is jealousy or the Bitch in His Head asking.

"Does fucking count?"

I get up and kneel on the bed facing him. I pull the teddy over my head and drop it on the bed. I caress my breasts. It feels so lovely to be touched.

"He did me in the aisle, Dimitri. Then he held me down so all the other passengers got a turn, too. You should have seen the dick on the captain."

"You're a fucking cunt, Alexa."

His hand clutches the belt so hard his knuckles have turned white.

I laugh again.

"You know my cunt belongs to you, and no one else, Dimitri. You know what a good girl I am."

I am a good girl. I am absolutely faithful to him and meticulous in my hygiene and I comply with all the Bitch's dictates, but loving him is hard work and sometimes I can't help teasing him.

His jaw is working like he is trying to hold the lid down on the steam that is boiling inside him.

"Tell me you know it, Dimitri. Tell me you know my cunt belongs to you."

His green eyes bore into mine.

"Your cunt belongs to me."

He drops the belt and reaches for the zipper on his pants.

There is always that moment before we fuck when Dimitri has to summon strength to trust me. After all, those medical tests were performed days ago. The Bitch might be whispering *what if's* in his ear right now.

He drops his pants and his cock stands out from his body as stiff as a steel girder. I don't know how he gets his socks off with it in the way, but he does.

He grabs my wrists in his big hands. He pulls my right hand to his nose.

"I smell your cunt on your fingers."

I spread my fingers wide for him, and he takes my pointer finger in his mouth.

The feel of his warm, wet mouth on my skin and the sight of my finger going in and out between his lips sends a lightening bolt to my cunt and makes me gasp.

He pulls me to him; his hand goes to the base of my skull, and he crushes his mouth against mine. We both groan. I press my breasts against his chest. His hands run down my back and dig into my ass, lifting me against him, the hard muscle of his cock sandwiched between our bodies.

"Oh, god, Dimitri, I've missed you!"

All my resolution leaves me, my veins are filled with mind-numbing desire for him. We kiss urgently, digging our fingers into each other's flesh.

He pushes me down onto the bed and presses my legs apart. He looks at my cunt, then dives into me with his tongue. I grab the sheets on the bed and hold on as he sucks me, bites me, fucks me with his tongue. He squeezes my thighs and pulls my skin still wider so that my labia are stretched. The pressure of his tongue is so delicious I whimper with pleasure. Thank god the Bitch likes the taste of my cunt.

Dimitri rises, his face wet with my fluid. He grabs my legs and rolls me back so that my knees are by my ears, my cunt completely open to him, ready to be penetrated. I know what is coming, but I don't care. All my planning means nothing now. He can pulverize me if he wants. I ache to feel his cock inside me.

But he doesn't enter me. His green eyes are not looking at

me. They're focused now on some point past my head. I twist and try to see what he is staring at. He is squeezing my legs so hard it hurts.

"What is it?" I whisper.

"The sheet." His voice quivers. It doesn't sound anything like his normal voice. "The sheet is untucked."

The fucking Bitch in His Head is talking now.

He lets go of me and pulls away. He stands up. His cock is still rock hard. He is trembling.

"The sheet..." he repeats. He looks dazed.

I sit up. I want to cry.

"I did that, love. Corbin asked me to make sure the bed was done up the way you like it. I'll fix it."

I roll to the side of the bed. I am shaking with anger at the fucking Bitch.

"I'll tuck it in. Don't worry. Everything will be fine."

I stand up and tuck the sheet in.

Dimitri's cock still makes a hard right angle, but there is a look on his face that unnerves me. He is only three years older than I am, but he looks like a weary old man.

I will do what I planned to do and I will fuck him and make him come, and the Bitch can go screw Herself.

"Shut your eyes and hold out your hands, Dimitri."

He scowls.

"No stupid games, Alexa." His voice is hoarse. "Get back on the bed and let me fuck you."

"If you don't shut your eyes and play nice, Dimitri, I'm leaving."

I have not threatened to leave him before. I'm not sure why I said it except the Bitch made me so angry. Dimitri stares at me. My threat has clearly startled him. He is much bigger and stronger than me and could easily force me to do what he wants, but he does not move.

"Please, Dimitri. I promise you that after we play my way, you can do what you want to me.

His mustache trembles. He shuts his eyes and holds out his hands.

I reach under the duvet, pull out the handcuffs, and snap them in place.

Dimitri stares at them like he can't believe what he is seeing. His cock, I am happy to see, is unfazed.

I fall to my knees and grab his hips in my hands and take the head of his fat cock in my mouth. I love sucking him. I lift one hand to play with the tender area under his balls, the other I move to his ass to push him deeper into my mouth.

Dimitri moans. The sound of his moaning, the way his eyes narrow with pleasure, is enough to raise the heat in my body and bring the juices back to my cunt. I pull my mouth away and stand up. His cock glistens with my spit.

I take hold of the chain that links the handcuffs and pull him to the bed.

He lies down in the center. He is breathing hard. His cock sticks up like a flagpole.

I take out the ropes.

"All silk," I assure him.

He arches one beautiful black eyebrow.

"After this, we play my way." His voice is normal now, but tense.

"Yes, I promise. Anything you want."

He watches with apparent detachment as I pull his arms over his head and tie the handcuffs to the brass rail of the headboard. I run my hands over his broad chest and belly. I kiss him deeply, our tongues slipping over and around each other like mating otters. His cock twitches. He stretches out his legs, no doubt anticipating my tying each ankle to the footboard, but that is not what I have in mind. I bend his left leg and bind his ankle to his upper thigh. I do the same for the right. Then I run ropes from the top of each thigh to the headboard.

I stand back at the foot of the bed and admire my handiwork.

"Do you like what you see?"

"Oh, yes, Dimitri. You're beautiful."

His cock rises up from his thick black swatch of pubic hair. The pink-colored cleft between his buttocks and the deep rose of his anus are exposed.

"Hurry up and do what you want so I can fuck you!" His voice is petulant.

I see the gap in my plan. The Bitch is lurking and could start issuing orders at any moment. Just as suddenly, I see the solution. I pick up Dimitri's silk tie from the chair and grab the panties that match my teddy. I will make sure I can't hear Her.

"Don't!" Dimitri says. He sounds panicky.

I ignore him and shove the panties in his mouth. He tries to spit them out but I hold his nose so he is forced to open his mouth. He snaps at me and tries to bite my fingers. I laugh and wrap the tie around his mouth.

His eyes bulge out slightly but he stops fighting me and lies back, trussed, silent, and compliant. He is all mine.

I stretch out on top of him, enjoying the sweet sensation as I rub my nipples against his chest. I turn his head and lick his ear and nibble down his neck and along his arms past the black hair in his armpits. I love the scent of his sweat.

I run my tongue down his belly, circle his navel, and push my tongue into it. His belly arches. He does not like this sensation, but I don't care.

I inch down his body until my mouth is at his cock.

I flick my tongue along the head of his cock and around the shaft and down around his balls. I would love to go farther and lick the tender skin around his anus but I'm afraid the Bitch in His Head would not let him kiss me later. I have to content myself with sucking his cock as hard and deep as I can.

I can hear groans and noises through Dimitri's gag. I stretch and reach under the pillow and take out my butt plug bouquet and the tube of lubricant.

"Surgical steel and brand new," I tell him. "Satin smooth and completely safe. Each has a nice wide handle at the end so it can't get lost inside you."

Dimitri utters some protests under his gag, but again I ignore him.

I take the smallest butt plug, not much wider than my pointer finger, and lubricate it. I squirt more lube on his tender pink puckered skin.

I have such a thrill watching the silver metal penetrate his ass. It slides in so easily. While I play with the plug with my right hand, I wrap the fingers of my left hand around the shaft of his cock and pump him like I am jerking him off. His cock is so engorged it is almost purple.

I pull the small plug out and drop it on my discarded teddy.

The next plug is a little thicker. Maybe the size of my two pinkie fingers combined. I can hear Dimitri's muffled groan when I push it in. I have a little bit of the sadist in me; his groan excites me so much I have to lean down and nip the tender skin of his inner thigh.

I suck his cock deeper down my throat as my right hand thrusts the plug in and out. Dimitri's legs tremble with each of my thrusts. I push the plug in and leave it there.

I pick up the largest plug. It is narrower than Dimitri's fat cock, but wider than three of my fingers combined. It is a hefty piece of metal.

I kneel between Dimitri's legs so he can watch me. I rub the head of the plug against my cunt like a dildo.

"It feels so good," I tell him. "Playing with you has made me so wet. I can slide it into me easily, Dimitri, but I don't want to be selfish. I got this for you. Besides, I'd much rather have your cock in me."

I drop the plug onto his belly. I move over him and straddle his waist. I hold the base of his cock with my left hand and rub it in circles against me.

"I want you so much, Dimitri. My cunt aches for you."

I am panting. I press the head of his cock hard against me. I would like to hold off longer, but I can't. My cunt is begging for him.

"I can't stand it. I have to put you inside me."

Dimitri's eyes are narrowed slits. He grunts through his gag.

I hold his cock still and push it into my body. I cry out when it fills me.

"Oh, that's good!"

I rock against him, enjoying the friction of his cock against the walls of my cunt. Waves of pleasure fill me. I look down and see the butt plug bouncing on his belly. I can imagine what it will look like stretching his skin, forcing open his narrow opening, and driving deep into his dark hole. I pick up the tube of lubricant and squirt the plug while it is still on his belly, drenching it and him.

I reach behind me and pull out the middle-sized plug from Dimitri's ass and drop it onto my teddy. I lift up the big plug. My hand is trembling. I look at my lover stretched out before me, his eyes shut, his head tilted back, his mouth slightly open beneath his gag, his chest rising and falling with his rapid breathing, his arms straining against his bonds. I can see the thick base of his cock where he enters me.

I realize that for the first time today, it is just the two of us in bed; the Bitch is nowhere in sight.

"I promise you, love, I will make you feel so fucking good. I promise you."

I reach back and position the big plug between his buttocks. I push gently against his anus.

I shove the plug into him in one hard push.

Dimtri throws his head back. I hear his muffled cry and see his jaw move under the gag.

The power I feel is like a narcotic flooding my veins. I pull the butt plug back and shove it in again. Dimitri's body strains and bucks under me, his head tosses from side to side, and he utters deep muffled cries. Nothing matters to me but fucking him like a wild thing. I dig my fingers into his waist and lean forward, pistoning my hips, and grinding my swollen clit against his pubic bone. Every thrust brings me exquisite pleasure. There is an explosive spasm that begins in my clit and spreads heat up the length of my cunt and makes my cunt muscles clutch Dimitri's cock and forces high-pitched cries of pleasure from my mouth. I am shaking like a rag doll and my cunt spasms again and I am still rocking my hips back and forth trying to sate my body's need.

"Uhh!"

Dimitri's face is contorted like a power lifter struggling to raise a tremendous weight above his head. Every muscle in his body is tense with his effort.

"Come!" I urge him. "Come!"

I churn my hips as hard as I can.

He grimaces and bellows and his head is thrown back and his mouth opens as wide as it can under the gag and his body trembles. I can feel his cock explode inside me. I rock against him until his trembling subsides and his animal cries stop.

I fall on him, resting my head against his chest for a minute. I'd like to stay there, but I know I can't. I have to clean up first.

I slip off of him and reach with shaking hands between his legs for the plug. His contractions have pulled it deep inside his body, and the wide handle is tight against his ass. I pull it out as gently as I can. Dimitri groans.

I wrap all the plugs in my teddy and carry them into the bathroom and put the bundle in a plastic garbage bag. My legs are unsteady, but I wash my hands several times with the antibacterial soap Corbin has supplied. I pick up two fluffy towels from the towel warmer and carry them to Dimitri. He is lying perfectly still with his eyes closed, his chest rising and falling with his shallow breaths. I untie his legs as quickly as I can and wrap his body in the warm towels. I untie the tie from around his mouth and pull out the wet wad of my panties. He doesn't say anything.

I unlock the handcuffs and tuck his arms under the towels. I slip into bed next to him and pull the duvet over us both. I rest my cheek against his forehead.

He pulls me close. He sighs deeply.

"That was good."

"Mmm," I agree.

"Next time, we do what I want."

"Yes."

"I'd love to fuck you in the ass, Alexa. I'd make you scream."

It will not happen. The Bitch in His Head will not let him.

I stroke his head until I hear the deep even breathing that means he is asleep.

Poor Dimitri. Lucky me.

SNUG DESIGNS

D. L. King

I loved the feel; loved the way the thin material conformed to the body and became a second skin. It was like a protective barrier, in a way. Rubber: It could show every curve, every crevice and bump you had in bas-relief but not allow access. It was a sort of tease. I loved the way it looked on women in clubs, and I got squishy-wet watching rubber fetish films. I was dying to wear some of my very own.

At a fetish party I spotted a woman wearing the most gorgeous black and blue latex skirt and heavy rubber corset. I introduced myself, told her how amazing she looked, and asked where she bought her outfit.

"I get all my latex and rubber from Mr. Snug."

"Mr. Snug? Never heard of it, where is it?" I asked.

"Mr. Snug is a designer." She told me he wasn't really any more expensive than the readymade stuff you could find on the racks at fetish stores, and sometimes you could be offered a real deal. "He'll only see you if you've been referred by someone he knows," she said.

We chatted for a while, and finally I worked up the nerve to ask if I could touch her corset.

"Sure."

I put my hand against her waist and squeezed. The rubber was heavy and had no give. It was black with deep blue trim. Blue accents set off her breasts by forming crescents under them. Blue lines of varying width with arrow points on them radiated out from the crescents toward the nipples, giving her tits a caged look. The corset was fastened with ten silver-buckled, blue rubber straps in back. She directed my hand down toward the bottom of the corset and onto the skirt.

The latex was smooth and hot. The sensuality of it took my breath away. I moved my hand toward her ass and stroked her curves.

"Um, this is so...I just can't stop..." I babbled.

She moved my hand to the front of the skirt and slid it down to her pussy. My fingers stroked and cupped her of their own volition.

"Honey, your eyes have gone out of focus," she laughed. "I'll talk to Mr. Snug tomorrow. You can call him in the beginning of the week; here's his card." She handed me a black, rectangular piece of hard rubber.

A few days later I arrived at a loft downtown. The top buzzer had a sign reading: SNUG DESIGNS, BY APPOINTMENT ONLY. I buzzed the intercom and heard a barked, "Who is it?"

After I'd given my name, the door buzzer sounded. I took the elevator to the top floor. It opened onto a loft, part work area and part display area. One wall was lined with mirrors. The windows facing the street were curtained.

"Hi. I'm Tim Snug. Grace tells me you have a rubber fetish."

I must have turned beet red because he said, "No, no, I love people with rubber fetishes. Without them, I'd be out of business. What can I show you today?"

Once I regained my composure, I told him I was interested in skirts. He ushered me over to a leather couch by the mirrored wall, and I watched him disappear into the clothing racks. While I began to ruminate on what a nice ass he had, he started talking.

"I like to make clothes to suit the customer, so most of my work is custom made. I keep some stock styles and sizes here in the studio to give my clients an idea of what I can do, but really, the sky's the limit." He came back out from behind the racks with half a dozen different skirts in almost as many colors. "You're about an eight, aren't you?" he asked. "Why don't you try on some of these; that way you can see what styles suit you best."

He led me to a large fitting room and explained how to try them on using talc to help them slide over my skin. The feeling was deliciously tight and confining, and when I came out to the main room to look in the mirror I was amazed how hot I looked.

Mr. Snug disappeared behind the clothes again, only to reemerge with a black fitted latex crop top, which he handed me. "Here, put this on. Your blouse hides the top of the skirt."

When I didn't come out of the fitting room right away, Mr. Snug entered. "Here, let me help you," he said. I was standing in the middle of the large space with my arms above my head, fighting with the tight top. One breast was half covered and the other was completely exposed, and just to complete the picture, my face was wrapped in the rubber.

"Mmmufflufled!"

"No, really, it's perfectly all right," he said. I felt baby powdered hands caressing my breasts. "It takes a while to get the hang of dressing in rubber." He gently pulled the bottom of the garment over my breasts and smoothed the straps over my shoulders. "Don't be embarrassed. This happens all the time." He pulled my hair out of the back and smoothed everything into place. His hands felt amazing on my tightly encased breasts. It seemed like he lingered over their swell a little longer than strictly necessary.

"See how the material shows the relief of your nipples?" As if to make sure I understood the question, he used both hands and allowed his fingers to slowly brush over each nipple simultaneously. "See how they poke up through the latex as they get more and more erect?"

I felt the most erotic full-body hug as I gazed at my reflection in the mirrors. Just thinking about the feeling of the latex encasing and conforming to my naked breasts gave me shivers, causing my nipples to become even harder. Looking in the mirror, I saw my hands slide up the sides of my breasts and pinch the nipples.

I was wearing a tight pencil skirt that fit like a second skin, and I couldn't help running my hands down my sides and over my rear. They slid their way to the front of the skirt and made their way up my body, back to the top where they caressed their way around my boobs and squeezed. My erect nipples naturally drew my fingertips to gently circle them before giving them another pinch and a little tweak.

"Ah...you do have a rubber fetish, don't you?"

I came back to myself immediately, but not before I noticed the slightly disheveled woman in the mirror with her mouth open and her eyes unfocused. "Oh, my god! I'm sorry! I didn't mean to..."

"No, no, that was very nice," he said, placing his hands on my hips. "It's refreshing, actually. So many of my customers are a bit jaded. Do you like the skirt?"

"Uh, yes, I..."

"Walk around, move in it. Sit. See if it's comfortable and if it suits you. You've still got several more styles to try on."

Eventually, between the two of us, I decided on two skirts, a fitted piece that belled out from my knees and came to midcalf, and a simple A-line. I chose silver-gray for the A-line and a combination of black and royal purple for the fancier skirt.

"Are you sure I can't interest you in a top?" he asked.

"Unfortunately, no. This is already more than I can really afford."

"All right then. Let me get your measurements. Did I notice a thong in the fitting room?" I must have given him quite a look because he quickly followed the first question with: "Because of the nature of rubber, I need to take my measurements in the nude, but if you have a thong, that will work, too. It's up to you."

I went back into the fitting room to change out of the last outfit I was wearing. While I put my T-shirt and underwear back on I thought about Mr. Snug's sleepy eyes and sensuous mouth. He had great hair and a nice ass. I could easily imagine running my hands over his naked body, or better yet, his rubber-clad body with, of course, an opening for his cock and balls. A while later, when I left his studio, these thoughts were still running rampant through my mind.

Two weeks later, I returned to pick up my new skirts. Mr. Snug was waiting for me as the elevator doors opened. He held out the two skirts for my approval.

"I think you'll really like these. Here, try the tight one on first," he said, showing me to the fitting room and following me in. "These are yours now. Don't use the talc; use the lube. Here, let me show you how. Take off your pants." He waited while I unzipped my jeans and stepped out of them. "No, no, you have to take your underwear off, too."

My eyes fixed on his mouth. I watched his lips form the words and didn't even think about what I was doing. I slid my thong down my legs and stepped out of it. I felt his hands smooth the silicone lubricant over my hips and thighs. He paused to pour more into his hands, and I felt them slide over my ass. The massaging sensation of his fingers and palms steadied and relaxed me. I could have thought about how I didn't know this guy who was running his hands over my half-naked body, but I didn't. I didn't even think about it when I felt the slippery hands make their way between my legs, from behind, caressing the crease of my thighs, on their way up over my pubic mound.

"Mr. Snug!"

"You feel nice and slippery now," he said. His arms were around my waist, and his hands were covering my bare pussy. "Let's get this skirt on you," he said as one index finger slid down the slit of my sex, grazing my clit, before sliding back out. He held the skirt as I stepped into it and pulled it up. It glided easily over my slick hips and ass. He zipped it in back and took a step away, as if to say, 'voila.'

Gazing in the mirror, I saw myself as truly sexy. The skirt completely suited me. It fit me like no other piece of clothing I owned. When I allowed my gaze to take in the whole picture, I saw a woman with flushed cheeks; moist, sensuous mouth, partially open; bedroom eyes, and skirt sure to make any man in the room fall to his knees. While I reveled in the sight of myself, I heard Mr. Snug over by the clothing racks.

"That skirt is perfect. I can't have you wearing it with that blouse though, I mean, the blouse is nice, but you'd look so much better in this." He held up a scoop-neck, latex top, in the same purple and black as my skirt.

"Ooh," I sighed.

"Would you like me to help you put it on?"

I bit my bottom lip and silently nodded my head. I watched in the mirror as Mr. Snug unbuttoned my blouse and removed it from behind. I watched as he unhooked my plain white bra and slid it down my arms, in front. I watched while he squeezed lube into his hands and rubbed them together before massaging the wet slickness into my breasts.

His fingers caressed, kneaded, and squeezed until I moaned. "Raise your arms." He slid the top over my head and arms and over my breasts, smoothing it down my sides. "There, now, that looks just about right."

It looked more than "just about right" to me!

"Now all you need to do is shine it up, and you'll be good to go."

"Shine it up?"

"Oh, yes! You can use the same lube to do that. Here, let me show you."

He poured more lube into his hands and smoothed them over every millimeter of the top. I had thought it looked great before but the shine added a whole other dimension to the material, making it look wet—like wet latex had been painted onto my body and wasn't dry yet—like shiny nail enamel for my body. The strength of his hands, sliding over my curves, made me hot, and my body was producing more than sweat now.

As he moved his hands down to the skirt, I shivered. He slowly shined the sides of the skirt, then the back, paying careful attention to my ass. Feeling the caress of his fingers against my skin, but not, was an amazing sensation. I knew he could feel every curve and crease but he couldn't feel the real thing, only the second skin covering it.

His hands moved to the front of the skirt and teased the flesh of my belly under the latex. Sliding both hands down in the form of a *V*, he sought out my mound. With fingers gently teasing the hot flesh, he slid lower, applying more pressure as he went. I leaned back, resting against his chest. My next-to-naked bottom could easily feel the bulge building in his pants.

I reached up and wrapped my hands around the back of his neck, stretching my breasts in the binding top while he continued to massage my sex. A finger strayed to the center and my slit. It burrowed inside, with the skirt as a barrier, and found my swelling clit. With his other hand, he reached down and slid the bottom of the skirt up to my mid thigh. Going no farther, he reached under and entered me with two fingers while his other hand was busy worrying my clit, over the rubber. All I could hear was the rush of blood through my body and the speed of my breath as it entered and left, entered and left. I felt the pressure build until I couldn't contain it any longer. The release started in my toes and spread up my body until it centered in my core, and I stiffened as I groaned my orgasm. He gently caressed my body until I'd caught my breath.

"Let me show you a fun way to take off your new rubber outfit," he said. He led me to his bathroom and turned on the shower. I unbuttoned his shirt and explored the hard chest underneath. I ran my fingers over his hard nipples and moved my hands down to open his pants. As I unzipped him, his cock fought for freedom inside his briefs. Unable to wait any longer, he pushed my hands down with his jeans and underwear.

He maneuvered us both into the shower; me fully clothed in rubber and him completely naked. His cock stood up proudly, and all I wanted to do was get my lips around it. He showed me how to remove my new clothes in the shower and as soon as I was naked, I pushed him up against the wall and sank to my knees under the spray of the water. His cock pulsed as I closed my mouth over it. I sucked and licked, first gently, then more insistently until I felt him begin to twitch in my mouth. Massaging his balls with one hand, I slid the other behind him. When he was ready, I pressed my finger just inside his ass to the sound of a very satisfying grunt.

I love to watch guys in the throes of an impending orgasm. I looked on as, eyes closed, head thrown back against the tile, mouth open and the most delicious sounds coming from him, his body begin it's race to the finish. When there was no turning back I caught his cock in my fist and removed it from my mouth so I could watch him come.

As I got ready to leave, he handed me a bag containing my purchases. He'd placed the wet skirt in a plastic bag and had folded my other new skirt with tissue paper, in a garment box. "Be sure to hang the skirt to dry when you get home," he said. I gave him my phone number in case he might need it later.

When I got home, I found he'd slipped the top into the bag too. There was a note: *This looked too good on you to take back. Maybe you'd better wear it when you come back to try on the A-line skirt; we'll need to check the fit on that one, too.*

COURTING HIM

Deborah Castellano

She leaned her head against the open windowpane and breathed as deeply as her corset would allow her. She loved this time of year, the way the birds sang outside and the explosion of cherry blossoms that brushed her cheeks if she leaned out far enough. She loved watching the ladies and gentlemen beneath her window seem to suddenly notice each other, furtively trading love notes and flowers after a long winter of hurrying past each other.

The boys that came to court her always oh so originally asked her...well, told her really, "Don't you want to be outside? See the big wide world?" Oh, they would take her to Paris, Milan, Athens, any place she (they) could possibly desire. She learned after the first young man (unimaginatively named Tom) that a thoughtful, detailed denial of such supposed desires only led to longer, more boring conversation. She learned quickly that it was best to stare into one's teacup that was thoughtfully laced with port by her dear lady's maid, Mimi, who was always there to glower at her suitors and chaperone her. This was inevitably misconstrued as modesty, restraint, and mystery by her gentleman callers.

The truth was, she had been what her father used to lovingly call fragile (in health at least) since she was very small. She had been fragile long before her father and mother passed away in a carriage accident when she was fifteen and she was handed over to her Master, a distant cousin whom she had never met before. She had never been well before, so how was she to know what she was supposedly missing? What was so great about outside anyway? If outside was so fantastic, why did people spend so much time indoors? She was worried when she first came to live with her Master those three years ago that she wouldn't be able to adjust to her new home and the new staff and...him. She never could have imagined in her grief-stricken haze that she would be lucky enough to live in a home as grand as his with a staff that was never anything but kind to her. She never could have imagined him. She leaned out the window farther to try to cool the blush from her face.

Besides being swooningly handsome (to her at least; bugger what those dolly mops in the ballrooms thought when they could be bothered to think at all) and well dressed, he was as smart as she was. That more than anything caught her. Gentlemen were generally so painfully dull, and the ladies, were just as bad. Both never seemed interested in discussing anything but who was betrothed to whom, which hat was best to wear for riding in the park, who was dabbing it up with whom, what cravat was the proper cravat to wear for what, what was the best method for hunting this or that, and a host of other tiresome subjects.

Not that he would notice her. Despite her endless stream of suitors, he never seemed to notice her charms. She would almost have started to think she wasn't fair of face if not for the constant barrage of compliments, flowers, and gifts thrust upon her. Certainly, he spent almost an endless amount of time in his study experimenting with one cure or another for her condition, with her dutifully at his side taking formulae notes and recording her reactions to his experiments. They spent hours playing chess, reading the paper together, debating Sappho, Molière, and even Austen. They discussed the garden's flora and fauna when he felt she was well enough. She liked these walks the best because it meant that she could lean on his arm and he would keep a hand on the small of her back protectively, which Mimi disapproved of.

Sometimes if she was patient, she could catch him out of the corner of her eye looking at her for far longer than was proper. This was always a double-edged sword, because these looks would mean that he would soon after shut himself into his study for long hours, taking meals alone there, or that he'd be going out on his own. As far as she could tell from collecting both empirical and circumstantial data from various sources, these evenings out usually entailed going primarily to his club where he would read the paper, drink too much brandy, smoke a few cigars, and play a few games of Hazard. He didn't seem to frequent brothels but occasionally would frequent ballrooms.

This drove her to dizzying heights of jealousy because he had only allowed her to learn to entertain in the drawing room, giving short recitals on the pianoforte or having tea with local ladies. He had deemed dancing to be too strenuous for her. She didn't really give two figs about being in an overheated, overcrowded ballroom with so-called gentlemen putting their hands all over her and attempting to look down her gown, but the idea of some other woman laughing up at him with his hands at her waist…it was too much to bear. It was worth it though, when he had walked in on John attempting to teach her to waltz several months ago, which seemed to entail primarily having him step on her feet and having to evade his attempts to kiss her. She had never seen her Master so angry. He forbid John from courting her further (which she didn't really care about) and forbid her learning to dance.

She was not one for tantrums, finding them beneath her, but something in her snapped when she realized she would never get to dance with *him,* and she sat on the floor and wept until she started coughing, and her maid had to find her a new handkerchief because hers was too vile and blood covered to use, and she was confined to her bed for three days. It was all the servants could talk about for weeks. But a week later in his study, he played music on his gramophone and taught her the waltz. He spun her around and around, and she thought she was the happiest girl in the world. Of course after that, he sequestered himself away for a week, but still…it was one of her best memories.

She sat on her window seat, idly stabbing at her embroidery, and thought dreamily of this morning. She was writing down the chemical composition for his newest elixir when she noticed her hair was falling out of its chignon. So she put down her pen and reached up to resecure her pins when she noted out of the corner of her eye that he stopped measuring the glycerin extract and seemed to be staring at her for a rather lengthy amount of time in a manner that could only be interpreted as brooding. She felt her heart speed up and willed her breathing to be even so as to not alert his suspicion that she had noticed him noticing her. Why wouldn't he just do something? She smoothed out her hair unselfconsciously and picked her pen back up. Of course he dismissed her after she finished writing the formula. Of course he shut his study door and would not come out for lunch. She sighed. What to do?

She spent the rest of her afternoon reading and daydreaming at her window trying to put together a plan. She examined the books that he allowed her to use for her own research and education, much to the shock of the staff. He had never allowed anyone to so much as dust them, let alone take them from his study, before she came to live with him. It was amazing that he was willing to spend so much time in her company, really. At five and thirty, he had been accustomed to a solitary household before she arrived. Nonetheless, her lady's maid indicated that he was bound for a ball this evening being thrown by a widow whom she knew for a fact had her eye on him. This would not do at all. She preferred subtlety over drastic actions, but she preferred him to not be in the arms of another woman more than anything. She knew she had an extra copy of his Henry Gray's Anatomy of the Human Body. She suppressed a rather large twinge of guilt and poured water all over the open pages, reminding herself that though the pages would be warped, they would be legible.

"Mimi?"

"Yes, Miss?"

"I want you to let it slip to the Master's valet that I ruined one of his books."

Mimi looked scandalized. "Miss, you know how he gets about his books! T'were I you, I would hide it and hope that he didn't notice it missing."

"Please, Mimi."

"All right, Miss," she said doubtfully.

She didn't have long to wait for a reaction. It would not be unlike him to wait until morning to scold her for her misdeeds, but in fact she was taking supper in her room and drinking tea when he strode into her room. She felt her heart beat far too quickly, so she quickly smoothed her face into the nonchalant expression she had practiced in the mirror before supper, as if she ruined precious books every day, and put her teacup down. She looked pointedly at Mimi, staring so hard at her she thought she would bore a hole through poor Mimi's skull. Mimi looked disapproving and reluctantly left. Mimi would only leave her alone with the Master and even then only reluctantly. She saw he was dressed for the ballroom, his cravat slightly askew as it tended to be unless she tied it for him, which couldn't happen when he was avoiding her. She felt her stomach sink and the bit of chicken in her tummy churn when she saw his dismay at the book. She took a deep breath. She needed to be steady and to see this through.

"I thought Miles was just gossiping," he said, carefully turning the pages in the book. "I'm very disappointed to see otherwise."

"My apologies, my Lord. I must have been distracted."

He looked bewildered. "What could have possibly distracted you enough to not notice you were ruining a text?"

"Theo proposed today." True. "And I told him to ask your permission for us to be married." Untrue.

Well. She received proposals every month or so, so that was

hardly anything exciting or inclined to make him delay his evening out. She always dismissed them out of hand whenever he mentioned some besotted swain who had decided after knowing her for all of six hours that she was marriage material. He never said anything to her past telling her who was interested, and she was always quick with her denial of interest.

"You...wish to marry Theodore?"

She looked closely at him. He appeared almost pale.

She made herself shrug. "I'm not getting any younger. He's as good as any."

"You're not...you're eighteen!"

She slowly moved closer to him to fix his cravat. "Is it a problem that I should be married, my Lord?"

He leaned back away from her slightly as she slid her hands carefully up over his chest and straightened his cravat. "You said you had no interest in being wed," he murmured. He looked at her expectantly, waiting for her to withdraw her hands from his chest. She didn't. She looked at him challengingly.

"Perhaps you haven't noticed, but I've grown into a woman," she said, drawing still closer to him, brushing her breasts across his chest.

His hands slipped around her waist and he pulled her still closer to him, almost against his will. "Is that what you want? To be married to...Theodore and warm his bed and have four of his children while he locks you away in the countryside so he can gamble away your dowry in gaming halls and bed his mistress? He would never care for you properly; he has no sense of how delicate you are."

"What else would you have me do?" she purred, leaning up

closer to him, inhaling the smell of him, a mix of parchment, ink, and leather.

She heard the tiny clink of her hairpins hitting the wood floor as he wound his hands into her hair and kissed her roughly. She felt her toes curling in her Magpie striped heels. This was far better than any of her other suitors' kisses and even better than trifle. She felt like her corset was crushing her because it was so hard to breathe, and she liked it. He pulled away from her abruptly and took a deep breath. "This is wrong. You are my ward. I am behaving improperly. My apologies. If it is your wish to marry…Theodore, then I will draw up the proper paperwork." He bowed.

"It is my wish to kiss you again," she said, looking at him directly. "I don't care about propriety, my Lord. Not with you, at least." She closed the space between them and wound her hands around his neck and reached up and licked at his jawline. She heard his breath quicken and allowed herself a moment of smugness. It was a good thing he didn't keep all the helpfully informative books hidden away from her. She slid her hands over his back like she had always wanted to. He kissed her neck and she arched up closer to him, finding that she was not the only one who was excited by this exchange. He swept her up carefully and sat her on her vanity table. Her skirts were pushed up around her thighs, and several bottles from the table rolled onto the floor, breaking. There was an explosion of rose, honey, and pale musk in the air. She ran her hands through his hair, tugging slightly. He kissed a line from her earlobe to her collarbone. She pulled off his waistcoat, sending buttons sliding across the floor. She reached down and reached under his tie to unbutton his shirt so she could feel his warm chest underneath. His heart was beating as fast as hers.

He inhaled the smell of her and she shivered.

"You're not well enough for this," he said softly.

"So you'll just have be careful with me," she replied, pulling him closer and kissing him. They explored each other's mouths and she couldn't help the soft moans escaping her, as their kiss became more passionate and rough. She loved feeling his hands glide over her body as carefully as if he was in his lab, but trembling slightly. His hands traced her breasts. Her brain felt covered in floss candy and she leaned her head back against the mirror. He kissed her neck, biting hard, making her purr as his hands covered her breasts through her chemise. He ran his hands over her hard nipples, pinching them just enough to make her gasp.

She shifted her thighs slightly, feeling how wet she was becoming. Noticing her shifting, his hands started stroking her stocking-clad thighs. She was having trouble breathing and forming any kind of coherent thought; all she could think was how much she wanted him. His hands found her soft, slick pussy and he gently parted her to stroke her clit with one of his hands. With the other, he quickly placed his fingers inside her and kept a rhythm similar to when they were waltzing. She moved on his hand quickly, grinding her hips against him. She heard her mirror bump against the wall and felt the bristles of her hairbrush digging into her ass. She knew she should try to keep quiet, but she couldn't seem to. Her breathing was loud and uneven; she tried biting the inside of her cheek to keep herself from making too many loud noises, but the longer he touched her, the harder it was to keep quiet. Her pupils were dilated, her hair was out of its pins, and her skin was flushed. She wasn't sure if this might indeed kill her but she didn't care. She could feel her orgasm building inside her, and just as she approached the edge, he slowed the rhythm of his hands.

"Look at me," he said, his voice rough.

"What! Why?" she cried. "Don't you dare stop!"

He smiled an intimate smile she had never seen before and felt her heart speed up even faster. "I didn't say I would stop, darling. I want to look into your eyes when you come."

She opened her eyes and looked at him, his shirt unbuttoned and his cravat askew. She looked into his eyes and as he touched her, she felt herself building again. She moved against him and watching him watch her just made her more excited. She felt the muscles in her thighs tighten and when he murmured, "You're so beautiful," she felt her back arch and she cried his name out and climaxed against his hands.

Her hands were shaking, and she fumbled with his trousers—too many buttons. He helped her strip off his pants and her hands found his hard cock. She cupped her hand around him and stroked him slowly, running her thumb over the tip of his cock. She gently massaged his balls with her other hand.

"Tease," he growled into her ears, breathing hard.

"Fair is fair," she purred. She teased him like this for several long minutes longer. "I want to feel you inside me," she whispered in his ear.

He shuddered against her. "I don't...want to take advantage...of you."

"Well, I want you to take advantage of me," she replied, pulling him closer, winding her hands into his hair.

He entered her slowly and gently and she sighed. He circled his hips and she moved against him, running her nails down his back and biting his neck. "All I can see is you," she said softly, feeling him thrust harder with her words. "Everything is gray without you," he said into her ear. She dug her nails deeper into his back and moaned his name, as his hands curled into her hair, pulling sharply. His thrusts became faster and he said her name into her neck as she felt him throb inside her. They stayed entwined in each other for a long moment.

"It appears I'm not going out this evening," he said bemusedly, surveying the wreckage in her room.

"It appears not," she said, grinning at him.

THE SECRET HISTORY OF LUST

Donna George Storey

No one was there.

Katie looked around the deserted shop, furtively, as if she were doing something naughty. For an antique store, it was unusually restrained in its offerings: two display cases stocked with jewelry, pocket watches, and silver tea sets, an alcove set up like a sitting room with a bookshelf of picture albums. Opposite, in what she immediately dubbed "the dress-up corner," a headless mannequin in a Roaring Twenties beaded gown stood sentry over a half-dozen other vintage dresses and men's jackets, which waited patiently on satin hangers for bodies to give them life again.

In the stillness, she could hear her pulse pounding in her ears. Katie knew she had done nothing wrong. Wasn't it practically her duty to step into a shop called Vintage Pleasures: A Trip to Yesteryear on the main street of the college town she would call home for untold years of scholarly toil?

And yet, as her gaze swept the room once again, she couldn't help likening this place to a virgin, slumbering in the daze of a white slaver's potion. Although she had no part in the dastardly abduction of the innocent soul, the pleasure of gazing at the girl's defenseless, succulent body was sinful violation enough. In the next moment, she fought down a less fanciful urge. With no one in sight, it would be too easy to pocket one of the ornate silver fountain pens arranged in a tray by the cash register and saunter back to her apartment.

Then, an even more disturbing vision flashed into her head—her naked body sprawled on her new futon as she masturbated in wanton celebration of her crime, one hand working her clit, the other sliding the purloined pen into the greedy lips of her vagina.

The grating sound of a key turning in an old-fashioned keyhole sliced through the silence.

Katie jumped, her guilt almost justified now. She considered slipping away before her presence was discovered, but raw curiosity kept her rooted to the spot.

Two men—one a tall, honey blond, the other a gray-beard who might be one of her future professors—walked out of a room at the end of the hallway behind the cash register. Through the open door, she glimpsed the glossy arm of a leather chair, a hint of green velvet drapery. Although it was high summer where she stood, she could swear she caught the scent of autumn wood smoke and a faint baying of foxhounds drifting from the room. Both men frowned when they saw her, but the younger one's expression quickly turned to a solicitous shopkeeper's smile. The "professor" took advantage of the distraction to make a hasty exit, a package wrapped in brown paper under his arm.

"May I help you find something in particular?"

The shopkeeper's tone was light, as if he expected her to say she was just looking.

Katie gave in to a new impulse—a desire to surprise him in turn. She gestured to the reading alcove. "Do you have any postcards from the nineteenth century? I'll be starting the graduate program in history here in the fall, and I'm always on the lookout for new research materials."

As she'd hoped, his eyes flickered with a new respect. "I do indeed. I have a good collection of vintage holiday cards and U.S. vacation spots from the 1850s through the 1960s. But my specialty is French postcards." He paused, eyes twinkling. "By which I really do mean pictures of Parisian landmarks."

Katie laughed, to let him know she got the racy reference, of course, but also to distract herself from the twinge of lust between her legs. She'd called it quits with her fuckbuddy when she moved a thousand miles away. A month of solo sex—with her vibrator if not stolen antique pens—had left her more vulnerable to this man's professional charms. Who knew what he might try to sell her?

"If that's your specialty, then naturally I'd like to see your collection. I spent a semester in Paris in college and it was wonderful." She felt her cheeks go warm. Why did she feel compelled to give him her full educational history? "By the way, I'm Katie. This is my first weekend in town, and I thought I'd check out the local shops."

"I'm glad you stopped in, Katie. I'm Alex."

He extended his hand and she shook it. His flesh was warm, pleasantly dry.

"Do let me know if I can be of service to you," he continued. "Many of the professors in town come to me with special requests. By the way, may I give you a welcome gift?" He turned to the tray of pens and selected one—a fairly thick specimen embossed with a sinuous floral design. "I've noticed history professors especially appreciate the sensual experience of using a classic fountain pen."

Again his eyes flickered, as if he knew what she'd been thinking moments before. Had he purposely added some opiate to the air to move his customers to lascivious thoughts?

No lady would accept such a gift from a stranger, yet despite the polite refusal forming on her lips, Katie's hand reached out and closed around the silver shaft.

In the hours to come she would indeed use the pen to pleasure herself, as if at his unspoken command. In the days to come she would do things with Alex she'd never done with another man, most of which he explicitly ordered her to do. No doubt there were countless junctures where a weakness of moral fiber led to her "degradation," but, in her memory, the chill of the metal on her fingertips marked the first and irrevocable moment of her fall.

Two weeks later, Katie was back in the shop. Or rather in the sloped-ceiling attic bedroom above the shop, straddling Alex's face. His tongue, as clever with cunts as with buttering up customers, was working such magic on her naked body that her lower half seemed to melt, filling his mouth to overflowing with her juices.

"Alex...I'm close," she panted. Her thighs were starting to

tremble, and she gripped the brass railing of the headboard to keep her balance.

He grunted, but then merely picked up the pace, lashing her clit like a jockey flogging his mount to the finish line.

Perhaps he hadn't heard? It was their first time to go beyond a lingering kiss, and she assumed he'd want to move on to more mutual pleasures. She pulled herself up and rocked back onto his chest.

"I'm ready," she said shyly. Even now, after several impromptu breakfasts at the local café and two official dinner dates, she felt a certain Victorian reserve around him.

"I know," Alex replied. "So climb back on and let me finish."

"Don't you want to...?" Katie faltered. Usually she swore like a sailor and yet, in here with him, she couldn't make herself utter the word *fuck*.

"It's not your place to argue. Get back in the saddle. And hold on to the headboard again like a good girl. Don't let go until you come." His voice was clipped and humorless, like a schoolmaster's.

Katie flinched. This was hardly what she was used to from a new lover, but she obediently scooted forward and closed her hands closed around the railing again. Her palms were slippery with sweat.

"That's a good girl. A good girl always does as she's told," he cooed, taking a breast in each hand and worrying her nipples with his thumbs.

Katie let out a moan. The praise made her feel naughtier, because she knew she wasn't good—not by the measure of yesteryear, which seemed to filter up through the floorboards from the shop below. For years she'd let men know her body without the sacrament of marriage. Far from renouncing her ways, this very night she was allowing a man she hardly knew to "gamahuche" her privates. All evidence suggested that she was very, very bad indeed.

Slut. Whore. Trollop.

The words echoed in her head; where they came from she didn't know.

As if on cue, Alex's hand glided around to her buttocks. After a brief, appreciative kneading of the soft flesh, he began to spank her—slowly, just enough to warm the skin and urge his filly on to victory.

Still clutching the metal railing, Katie felt her body shudder and twist with each blow, hot shame knotted with prickling desire. She was bad. He knew it and he was punishing her, as she deserved. The moan became a long, low groan as her orgasm gathered in her belly. A few more flicks of his tongue on her swollen clit and she was gone, her hands knocking the headboard rhythmically against the wall to the beat of her contractions.

Afterward he held her, stroking her hair.

"Can I do something for you?" She cupped his erection poking up through his khakis. He was still fully dressed.

"Don't feel any obligation."

"I'd like to," she pressed.

"I'm fine. I enjoyed it very much." Indeed, his voice was lazy, content.

"You're making me feel guilty, as if I've eaten up all the dessert." She meant to sound teasing, but her tone had a touch of desperation. Didn't he want her?

Alex smiled and pulled her closer. "Think of it this way—haven't there been times when a man's taken his pleasure and left you high and dry? Consider this my way of making it even."

She had to laugh. Historically speaking, she was indeed a few orgasms in the red, but she couldn't quite believe his reluctance was pure generosity. Obviously he could get it up—the tent pole in his trousers lingered on—but there might be other complications. She remembered his frown the moment he walked out of that locked room with another man, as if he'd shown her a glimpse of something she was never meant to see.

She wanted to see it all now.

"By the way," she said sweetly, snuggling into him, "I've been wondering for a while...what do you keep in that back room downstairs?"

His body stiffened. At last, it seemed, she'd touched him. "It's just a collection of things for special customers I think best not to display in the store."

His fastidious answer made her bolder. "Does it have to do with sex?"

His laugh was almost a snicker.

So it was a ridiculously obvious question—her next move was obvious, too. "Well, when do I get to see it?"

"I'm not sure it would interest you. It's not part of the shop. It's more of a club. For gentlemen."

"No lady can be a member? Do I have to bring a lawsuit for gender discrimination?" She wrinkled up her nose to show him it was—mostly—a joke.

"I'm doing nothing illegal, by the way." His voice was calm, but she felt him draw away, an almost imperceptible shift of his body on the bed. "But my collection represents the sensibility of an earlier time. Modern women tend to find much of it offensive."

"I probably know the nineteenth century better than you do, and I'm pretty open-minded about sex. I have quite a collection of erotica. Vanilla, lesbian, gay, it all turns me on." She propped herself up on one elbow and smiled down at him. If he and the gray-beard did more than wrap packages in that room, it was probably best to coax it from him now.

"I've acquired some material involving homosexuality, but my main focus is *filles de joie*." He seemed to be making a special effort to look her straight in the eye. "My side specialty is discipline. It's not for everyone and I want to protect both my customers who enjoy such things and those who don't."

Now his stiffness was starting to annoy her. "Alex, I just sat on your face while you spanked me and bossed me around like a young master toying with the novice parlor maid. And I liked it. A lot. Don't you think I seem like a promising candidate for your club?"

He admitted her point with a smile. "There's an initiation. To establish that...you're one of us."

"Do I have to pee standing up? I can probably manage it with practice."

Alex smiled. The saucy, spirited approach seemed to be working. "Well, it will have to be different from the usual gentleman's agreement. I'll try to come up with something appropriate. But then you'll have to see if you're up for the challenge."

The way he said "appropriate," soft and slow, made her cunt muscles clench.

And the "challenge"? He'd learn soon enough she'd do whatever it took to get what she wanted. Now more than ever, she wanted to get inside that secret room. Not so much as a member but as a phantom spy, to watch men of consequence as they sipped port, fondled cigars, and studied the latest portraits of coupling nudes from Paris. Gentlemen all, they would ignore any restless shifting of the weight on the leather couch, any instinctive moistening of mustachioed lips, certainly any sign of tumescence beneath a custom-tailored dinner jacket. But Katie would see and, unable to restrain herself, she would reach out to coax their poles from their trousers and stroke the tender, pink satin caps with her ghostly fingers until they erupted in Vesuvian fountains of spunk.

She realized with a start that Alex was studying her face intently.

Katie blushed. From the beginning, he seemed to see right into her most secret thoughts. Yet to her he remained closed, locked, like a heavy oak door.

Katie had hoped Alex would open the room to her the next day, but he put her off indefinitely while he devised her initiation. The test must be just right, he insisted, and her patience would show her sincerity.

At last, one full week later, she found herself knocking on the door of the darkened shop at ten in the evening. She was wearing the prescribed outfit: a light-colored blouse and dark skirt. No panties, no panty hose. Alex had allowed that a pair of thigh-highs would do to keep her shoes from chafing her feet, but he insisted her hair be pulled back in a braid and tied with a "girlish" ribbon.

This was, officially, the second phase of the initiation. For the first, Alex had asked her to find a passage in a book, from something published before 1940, that she found especially arousing. Katie tackled her assignment with the seriousness she brought to her first week of classes—and indeed, she cared more about pleasing Alex than any of her real professors. She had a few volumes of Anaïs Nin, of course, but she rejected that choice as too predictable. Fortunately, while unpacking her books that had recently arrived from the shipping company, she happened upon Colette's *Claudine in Paris*, and remembered a scene where the feisty heroine discovers her old school friend, Luce, is being kept by a rich, old relative. Gradually Claudine forces her friend to confess that the old lecher makes her act out his sexual fantasies in return for jewels and as many petit fours as she can eat.

The passage was more sly insinuation than explicit porn, but filling in the blanks with her own fevered imagination made Katie hot enough to pleasure herself afterward. With visions of the tantalizing secret room fueling her, she quickly copied out the pages in neat cursive on cream-colored stationery and sent it to him with a dab of sealing wax on the envelope, just as Alex had instructed.

Two days later, he called to inform her that her application had been accepted and she would be granted a personal interview the next evening.

He was waiting at the door in waistcoat and jacket when she arrived.

"Please step over there," he said, like a butler, his eyes sweeping over her outfit. He gestured to the reading alcove, which was now blocked from the view of the street with an Oriental folding screen. A single lamp glowed golden through the rice paper.

Obediently slipping behind the screen, Katie discovered Alex had replaced the comfortable armchairs with a nicked wooden desk and a small chair more suitable for a child. Laid out on the desk were a ruled notebook and a fountain pen.

"Sit down," he said.

Katie sat.

"As you know, the Vintage Pleasures Gentleman's Club is making a special exception in considering your application for membership. In order to protect the confidence of our members, we require written evidence of your like-mindedness. To be blunt, we require a document that can be used against you in public should you decide to break our rules of utmost secrecy. In other words, the damage to your reputation must equal the damage to ours."

Katie's eyes widened. She was hoping the initiation would involve sex, even mild humiliation, but she wasn't sure she was ready to endanger her professional "reputation." And yet, the thought made her breath come faster.

"With that in mind, the next step in the application process is for you to write an essay in your own hand describing an erotic scene involving young Luce and her guardian. You will then write a pledge that this is your original work and sign it. Is this amenable to you?"

Katie exhaled quietly. His challenge wasn't as bad as she feared. And yet, she wouldn't want such a document to get into the wrong hands. It was a clever choice to secure her silence.

She nodded, then added, "Yes, sir."

"Very well. You have half an hour. If the essay is not sufficiently explicit or imaginative, your application will be denied." He placed a pocket watch on the table, then turned and disappeared behind the screen.

Katie stared at the watch, her pulse outpacing the steady ticking of the old timepiece. She had plenty of material gathered from years of turgid fantasy to write a dirty story. But the schoolroom setting brought back another lesson—the teacher's favorite topic always brought a better grade. Alex had set the stage. All she had to do was dramatize the scene where the frog-faced uncle-in-law forced Luce to write a theme, dressed in a pinafore, before he presented her with her latest trinket. In Katie's private version, pretty Luce had one more task to perform before she received her final reward: she must let her guardian give her one smack on the buttocks with his riding crop for each mistake, after which she must utter not a word of protest while he mauled her breasts with blue-veined hands and forced his preternaturally vigorous erection into her tender folds.

To Katie's surprise, the words flowed easily, so easily she blotched the paper with ink several times and had to cross out a few clauses that seemed too trite. Still, she had four pages of pure smut ready when Alex reappeared, his eyebrows lifted in expectation.

He took the theme book, perched himself on the desk, and proceeded to correct it with a red pencil. She thought he seemed to take rather too much pleasure in making marks all over the pages, but when he looked up, he was smiling. "This is excellent work."

"Do I get to see the naughty room now, Schoolmaster?" she said, giving him a mischievous smile.

"All in good time," he replied, his reserve unruffled. "First, as you yourself suggest in your essay, it is important that young scholars be held accountable for their mistakes. I've counted twelve instances of sloppiness and improper grammar. That's twelve smacks on your naked buttocks—I don't have a crop, so I hope a palm will do—after which we will conclude with the final requirement."

"There's another one after this?" Katie's voice came out in a small squeak. The sudden tingling in her ass made it difficult to speak.

"I'll need several photographs of you for our records. Nude or partially nude—that part doesn't matter. But it must be clear that you are masturbating."

Katie brought her hand to her chest, rather like a Victorian miss with overly tightened stays. Erotic writing was one thing, but making her pose for amateur porn might just test her limit. Shocked, she blurted out, "Is that what you make the men do?"

"That information is available only to members, I'm afraid. Of course, if that's too much for you, we can terminate the proceedings right now."

Is that what he wanted all along? She met his stern, steady gaze. He would not relax the requirements, she could tell that much, but she also saw a glimmer of warmth in his eyes that heartened her.

He wanted her to pass the test.

And she did, too.

She stood and began to unbutton her blouse. "Would you like me to bend over the desk for my 'corrections'?"

He couldn't restrain a smile. "That will do nicely."

Draping her shirt and bra over the chair, Katie shimmied out of her skirt. She leaned over and rested her elbows on the table. The cool air teased her bare skin; the cuffs of the thigh-highs seemed tighter, like bonds. She tilted up her ass to show she was ready.

Alex cleared his throat. "Count them out together with me."

His palm met her flesh.

"*One.*"

Their voices echoed in unison.

Katie noticed her chest was already mottled with arousal.

"Two."

As before, his blows were not particularly hard. They seemed rather to remind her of her submission, her depravity, her willingness to strip and offer her flesh to any sensation her master might deal her.

"Three."

"Alex?"

"Is this too much?" His voice was suddenly soft with concern.

"No. But I...I wonder if you could spank me right on my asshole. I...I like that."

He made a strange sound in his throat. "Yes, that would make the punishment more effective. Spread your legs wider."

Four, five, six.

She whimpered.

"Your back is all flushed." He paused to run his hand along her flank.

She wiggled her ass, puppylike, impatient for more.

The second six fell quickly, a series of sharp slaps on her anus that left her so aroused she could barely babble the numbers.

"Sit on the desk now," he ordered hoarsely.

She turned and wiggled up onto to the table, her ass smarting deliciously.

He moved in between her legs and kissed her, hard.

"Take the pictures now, please," she begged, her breath ragged. "I'm so turned on, I'll masturbate here, on the desk, like a naughty schoolgirl."

"Fuck the pictures, I want you now."

"Here? Do you have a condom?"

"I've got some in the room," he said, grabbing her elbow and pulling her down the hall.

The door was half-open. A single green-shaded lamp gave the room a twilight glow.

The first thing she saw was a wide leather sofa. He pushed her back onto it and arranged her legs, one bent against the back, the other splayed over the cushion.

While he fumbled for condoms in the end table drawer, Katie glanced around the room, furtively, not quite sure she had the right. One look sufficed to let her know she was in a temple to fleshly desire. Above the fireplace was a watercolor of a woman draped over a chaise, touching herself between her legs. On the mantle was a copy of the famous Pompeian sculpture of Pan coupling with a she-goat. The other wall boasted framed black-and-white photographs of nude women gazing into the camera with strangely blank faces, their plump thighs parted, although their labia were mostly obscured by thick bushes of dark hair.

Alex was above her now, his trousers at his knees; his thick, red cock in its raincoat, poking toward her.

"I look like one of those French whores," she said, nodding at the portraits.

"You do," he admitted. "I'd like to photograph you this way. Later."

"Then I'll feel like one, too."

"Is that bad?"

"Not in here," she said, drawing him toward her, sighing as he slid inside, as his balls tickled her sensitized asshole with each thrust. He came inside her quickly, like a john, but she didn't mind his selfishness. It made her feel good to give him pleasure.

Besides, she owed him one.

Afterward, he lent her an antique kimono to throw over her shoulders while he gave her a quick tour of the club. There were barrister bookcases filled with multiple illustrated editions of *Fanny Hill,* a slim volume called *Blushing Bottoms,* collections of erotic prints from China and Japan. He showed her a stereoscope with a stack of cardboard slides including a series on courtesans of Morocco and a scene of a woman in congress with a pony. His collection of old vibrators with thick, superannuated cords made her shiver—shocking, no doubt, in the most literal meaning of the word.

He waved his hand around to the dozen other drawers and cabinets, guarding secrets within secrets. "Anything special you'd like to see tonight?"

She hesitated. "What's your greatest treasure?"

It was the right question. He smiled and walked to a writing desk, unlocking it with a key he produced from his pocket. He took out a small wooden box. They sat down on the sofa together and he opened it. Inside was cradled a slim object, the size of his palm, wrapped in soft cloth.

Secrets within secrets.

As she watched, breath bated, he unwrapped the bundle to reveal a tooled leather case and opened the latch. Through the protective glass, a woman, no doubt another *fille de joie,* stared out at them with dark, velvet eyes. She was nude, except for a bridelike gossamer veil draped over her head and shoulders.

"This is from the eighteen-forties."

"The dawn of modern pornography," Katie observed.

"Yes. This is how it all started."

"She's so voluptuous," Katie murmured, noting the generous curves of the model's belly and thighs.

"We don't see many erotic pictures like this now. Models are airbrushed and starved, but I imagine real bodies look pretty much the same. Photographers weren't afraid of flesh back then. They weren't afraid of reality. They celebrated it."

He gazed at the daguerreotype like a man in love.

Katie felt a flicker of jealousy. "How much is she worth?"

"I'm not sure I would sell her to anyone. It wasn't easy to get hold of one in such good condition. A hundred and fifty years ago it was the same. A man had to go through many trials to earn possession of these ladies."

"Trials do make the final reward sweeter."

"Yes." He acknowledged her with a quick smile, but his eyes were still fixed on the naked woman resting in his hands. "That's why this is a treasure. But for me it's more than that. It's a doorway to the secrets of the past, to a time when sex meant something. Now it's cheap. Back then there were consequences. Sacrifices."

"Mostly for women," she added.

"No, for a man of conscience as well. A true gentleman would not take his responsibilities lightly."

She'd never seen him speak so passionately.

"I'm not sure I miss those days. I'd only be admitted to this place as a whore, not an honorary gentleman. Now I can be both."

Finally he met her eyes. "So, is this what you expected?"

Katie paused, aware of her new privilege. For the first time since they'd met Alex was vulnerable to her judgment, her desire.

"That's a difficult question to answer. But I am glad I passed the test."

He smiled, his relief obvious, and draped his arm around her shoulder. "I'm glad I didn't disappoint you. I like to keep my customers satisfied."

His hand cupped her breast, tentatively, through the silk robe, and she yielded, leaning into him with a sigh. There was time for more words later. Time to confess that now she'd earned entrance to the secret room, she was hungrier than ever. She wanted to know it piece by piece, have him introduce each treasure like an old friend; recount its story, its charms, whether it moved him to jerk off, or whether he needed to be punished for thinking such naughty things. She knew she wouldn't be satisfied until she learned every secret in this room.

The secret history of lust.

PASTA WITH BLUE CHEESE AND ANAL

Ms. Naughty

The blue cheese melts on my tongue, sharp and creamy at the same time. I close my eyes and savor the luscious sensation of the flavor, a blush of wrongness combined with heavenly cream. The taste sends a shiver through me, making my ass clench briefly around the slim butt plug.

I smile. Tonight, as my anniversary present, Stephan will fuck me in the ass.

I am fussing around the kitchen, making the evening's special meal, pasta with blue cheese and asparagus. It's hard to keep my mind on the job because my anticipation of tonight's debauchery is seriously distracting. All I can think about is sensation.

I'm supposed to be cutting up the blue cheese but instead I'm eating it, slipping slivers of yellow delight into my mouth, letting it rest there while the flavors slowly dissolve, and then washing it down with a sip of bold cabernet sauvignon.

Yes, *bold* is the word for this wine, if not downright aggressive. It's the kind of wine that would hold you down and fuck you hard without preamble, if it were a man. But it suits the cheese perfectly, and I am in a gourmand's heaven.

I never used to like blue cheese. I remember my first taste of it as a young girl, tentatively biting into a small slice from a party platter. I remember how the strong taste overwhelmed my inexperienced senses, and I promptly spat it out in horror. It took years, many years, before I was willing to try it again, and even then I had to work hard at enjoying it. Slowly, the juxtaposition of bitterness, sourness, and delightful cream won me over.

I never used to like anal sex either.

I've heard it said that women will try anal sex twice: once to see what it's like and a second time to see if it really is that bad. I used to be one of those women.

The first time I ever tried it was in college. I was young and stupid—par for the course. I offered up my ass after much impassioned prompting from my then-boyfriend, Dennis. There was no preparation, no lube, no pleasure at all. What was more awful than the cringing pain and fervent wish for the fucking to be over was the fact that I collapsed into tears afterward, turning my face to the wall. I remember Dennis worryingly stroking my brow and apologizing fervently, but I couldn't speak. I'd been a willing participant, eager to try something new, but it was a sordid loss of that particular virginity, one that left me feeling violated and strangely sad.

From then on I was certain that anal was something men

wanted but women shouldn't offer. What was the point, after all? Guys seemed mad for it, if only so they could boast about it to their friends. What sane, pleasure-loving woman would want to stick a cock in her ass?

Stephan changed all that.

Beautiful, serious Stephan, the love of my life. Stephan with his wry smile, sharp mind and a tongue to match, a thin man with the weight of the world on his shoulders and the light of mischief in his eyes. He too is an acquired taste, just like the blue cheese—just like anal. As with all difficult pleasures, he is absolutely worth the effort.

Stephan opened the crack, as it were. He began my anal innings by gently touching my butt during a particularly rampant session of cunnilingus. There I was, writhing like a pleasure-stricken octopus as he expertly tongued my swollen clit, my hands grasping my forehead, my breasts, and then his head, pushing him into my cunt with glee. Suddenly he touched a finger to my ass, wriggled it. The shock of it—and the distinctly pleasurable sensation—sent me into spasms, complete with neighbor-annoying squeals.

Afterward he looked me straight in the eye and said: "Have you ever been fucked in the ass?"

I flushed, suddenly filled with an unidentifiable shame, and I couldn't meet his gaze.

"Well?" he asked.

"Once," I admitted, quietly. "In college. It really hurt."

"Mmm," he said, nodding; unsurprised, perhaps. His dark eyes held mine, considering.

"What? What about it?" I felt my face grow hot, ready to be offended for no reason whatsoever.

"That's unfortunate," he said, his tone tinged with pity.

I don't like to be pitied in bed.

"Unfortunate," I snorted. "Yes, it is, isn't it? Anal is just a stupid thing girls do to make guys happy. It's what you do when you want to pretend to be a porn star—bend over and take it up the ass like a good girl! And it's not natural. There's a perfectly decent cunt right there so why would you fuck someone's butt? I wish I'd never tried it, that's what I wish. I was just trying to make my boyfriend happy in college when I did it. Big mistake."

"You know there are women who enjoy anal," Stephan said quietly.

"Yeah, right," I said. "And they get paid by the hour for it."

"You liked it when I touched you there tonight."

"That's different."

"How?"

"You were just shocking me into getting off."

"Are you sure?"

"I don't like anal."

"It's an acquired taste, you know."

"No way are you fucking my ass, Stephan."

He smiled, his expression more than a little condescending, but he said nothing more. The conversation stopped there, and we didn't explore it further for some months.

Indeed, it was me who initiated it again as we lay languid on the tangled sheets, our sweat drying after a long Sunday afternoon fuck fest.

"So, how many times have you done anal?"

Stephan looked sideways at me, but didn't blink. He answered with a matter-of-fact tone. "I don't know. Probably too many times to count."

"Who with? Sherie?" I couldn't keep the bitchy tone out of my voice when I said her name.

"No. She was too uptight for that. Wouldn't let me anywhere near her ass."

I decided to ignore the "uptight" reference. "Who then?"

"A girlfriend from a while ago. You don't know her. She just liked anything anal, so I was happy to oblige."

"I don't understand how any woman can actually ask for it."

Stephan reached up and gently circled my lips with his forefinger. "She knew how to do anal properly, so it was always good. And she taught me the right way too, so it never hurt her. It was never like when you did it in college that time. She always had massive orgasms when I fucked her ass."

I couldn't help it—my pussy clenched when he said that.

"She...she actually came?"

"Oh, yeah. She always said her orgasms were better during anal."

I found myself wondering how a woman could possibly come if she had a dick in her ass. It didn't seem right. Was there some kind of trick to it? Or was she just some kind of freak?

"How do you do it properly, then?" I asked, curious in spite of myself.

Stephan shrugged. "Patience, lube, a vibrator. Maybe a butt plug. The most important thing is that the woman has to want it and enjoy herself, otherwise it's pointless. Anal sex is always about the woman's pleasure."

I'd never thought of it that way.

"And it helps if you're in love with each other, of course."

I looked at him, expecting that last comment to be cynical somehow. His expression, however, was completely guileless.

He really meant it.

Again, my pussy squeezed involuntarily.

For a week afterward I couldn't stop thinking about our conversation, turning it over in my mind. I wondered if I was being too closed-minded about the whole business. Maybe I was denying myself something that might be pleasurable, something that might enhance my relationship with Stephan. The idea of anal sex was still frightening, but I realized that what he'd said was comforting, somehow. Stephan was good in bed, no doubt about that. Perhaps this was something he'd also be good at.

So one day, alone with my vibrator, I decided to do a little experimentation. After a few minutes of standard clit stimulation I moved Ol' Faithful down to my ass, tentatively touching the tip to my closed pucker. I groaned in spite of myself—it felt good! Spreading my legs wide, I manually rubbed my clit and let the buzzing plastic of the vibe probe against my anus. Soon I found myself wanting to push it inside but my mounting orgasm arrived in a fury and I never got that far.

The day after that I combined Ol' Faithful with my Hitachi Magic Wand and damned near hit the roof.

I then asked Stephan to help me experiment a little more.

"You want me to do...what?" he blurted, nearly dropping a bottle of expensive white.

The kitchen probably wasn't the place to spring it on him.

In any case, he was eager to educate me. We had some amazing fuck sessions, just him, his fingers, my ass, and my vibes. I couldn't help but be stunned at how easily my asshole would relax when I was turned on. He'd lick and tickle me into a frenzy before getting to work on my butt, teaching me to welcome the new and satisfying sensations. Bit by bit, the fear retreated, replaced by a wondrous desire to explore my own body. I found myself getting turned on by the very idea of anal sex, daydreaming about it at work, my panties dampening during business meetings.

Soon, I was ready to be fucked in the ass.

And the first time we did it, I cried.

This time, however, it was tears of joy, an outpouring of sheer emotion. The pleasure of the act was new and exciting, but the intimacy of the thing overwhelmed me. I'd opened up and shared something secret with Stephan, something profoundly personal and joyful. We both leapt into a sea of sensation, just the two of us floating in pure animalistic sexual awareness, our orgasms teetering delicately at the edge, ready to send us into oblivion. It was better than I'd ever imagined.

Anal became a special thing for us, an opportunity to reconnect with each other, to indulge in absolute no-holds-barred sex without barriers, a meeting of souls.

It sounds mad, I know. How can anal sex be a spiritual thing? For certain it's not something they encourage at Catholic marriage counseling.

I don't care though. Anal is what we do, and we do it with love, every time.

Tonight I'm just as eager and excited as that first time. Stephan will be home any minute, and our special celebration will begin. I've managed to salvage some of the blue cheese for the pasta, and the meal is almost ready. I take another sip of red wine and swirl it around my mouth, thinking about the fun I had slipping in my butt plug. It's there now, tight and secure, getting ready to make way for Stephan's hot cock.

He arrives a little late, closing the door quietly behind him in his usual careful way. His hassled post-work expression dissolves when he sees the way I'm dressed—suspenders, corset, silk panties, the whole shebang. Within seconds I'm in his warm embrace, his lips pressed urgently against mine. He reaches a hand down to my asscheek and grabs a handful of flesh. The subsequent jiggling of my butt plug makes me moan involuntarily.

I pour him some wine and serve out the meal, the table immaculately set with silverware and candles. The food is perfect, and I'm proud of my efforts in the kitchen, but I can't give it the attention it deserves. Stephan is teasing me.

"Did you masturbate today?" he asks.

I giggle coquettishly, playing the game. "Of course not. I've been waiting for you."

"Not even when you were pushing that lovely butt plug into your ass and fucking yourself with it ever so slowly?"

"Well...maybe just a little."

"Did you come as you were playing with your ass?"

"I didn't really come. Not very much."

"Did you wish my cock was sliding into you, pounding you so hard that you begged?"

We don't finish our dinner.

Stephan leads me hurriedly to the bedroom, stripping off his clothes with ease. The sight of his wiry muscled body and thick cock turns me on, as always. He bends me over the bed so my ass is sticking up in the air and gently eases my panties down. The bright pink silicone base of the butt plug nestles between my asscheeks, and I know seeing it makes him eager to fuck me.

Stephan reaches over to the nightstand, and I feel a cool trickle wallowing down the crack of my ass. He rubs the lube all over and I sigh. His hands are always warm.

"Get the Hitachi. I want to play with you," he says. I obey, reaching under my pillow to where the electric vibe lies, waiting and ready. The throbbing vibrations against my swollen clit make me moan, but I'm already anticipating what comes next.

Stephan slips two fingers into my cunt and then jiggles the base of the butt plug. The combination of sensations is exquisite, and I feel like I could come immediately. No doubt about it, I'm now such an expert at butt-fucking I can orgasm at the drop of a lube bottle. A part of me is amazed at how far I've come. As it were.

Stephan gently pulls the butt plug out and then plunges it inside again, fucking me with the toy. He has an innate knowledge of what I need and how much force I want, never going beyond the boundaries of what I can take. I love him for that.

Tonight I feel ready for strength, for lashings of hardness and animal lust. I love butt-fucking because it makes me feel wanton and depraved, like a slut with no time for common decencies. For a short space of time I become a woman far removed from the everyday, a lustful goddess who will do anything and say anything to get what she wants.

My butt feels incredibly flexible, like I could be fucked by a fence post. When Stephan removes the butt plug I'm more than ready for his cock. Even so, the thick bulbous head feels enormous against my asshole. He holds there for a second, just touching me, and I feel ready to explode. I want it, and I want it now. The vibe continues its work as he gently pushes his cock into me, slick skin inching slowly past my willing muscles. I groan as I feel him slide into me, pushing the shaft home. I can feel everything—and it feels wonderful.

Slowly the fucking begins, a gentle rhythm of relentless pleasure, Stephan gripping my hips as his moves his piston cock in and out of my flesh with a sureness that I adore.

"Please," I whimper. "Harder."

He obeys, increasing his speed inexorably. I grind the vibe into my clit, awash with glorious pleasure, emitting deep, animalistic grunts with each thrust of his cock. I'm lost now, a slave to my growing orgasm, impossibly aware of every nerve and every rippling tide of joy.

And he's there with me, urging me along, sharing in the moment and the delight of it all. We're joined in every way, he and I, like lost souls sanctified at a depraved communion, made pure by reptilian lust. I can't think of anywhere else I'd rather be than here, right now, with Stephan's cock plunging in and out of my asshole.

I come. The orgasm arrives and overwhelms every sense and every emotion. A point of shimmering, white light appears before my closed eyes, a beacon of pure pleasure illuminating my brain as the waves of ecstasy spread out from my cunt and my ass. I scream, I shake, and I ride the climax to its last quiver.

Stephan is seconds behind me. My clenching ass milks him dry and he shudders against me, low gasps punctuating each breath.

We cuddle together on the bed, exhausted but utterly satiated.

"Happy anniversary," Stephan says eventually, and I kiss him and hold him tight.

"I'm so glad I found you," I say, putting a lifetime of longing and love into my embrace.

And then I get up and put on my robe.

"Where are you going?" Stephan asks.

"I'm hungry," I say. "And my blue cheese pasta is too good to waste."

CARDIO

Elisa Garcia

I am mesmerized by Pablo's hips.

And abs.

And thighs.

And tight, tight ass.

But nothing compares to those sinuous hips shaking fluidly, sensually, hypnotically side to side in front of me.

Salsa beats blare through the studio, and the dozen or so women flanking me seem every bit as entranced as I am watching Pablo. Together we stare as, toes perfectly pointed, he executes a rapid jump-kick combo the likes of which I've never seen outside a Miami club. Sweat streams down his back. His thin nylon shirt clings to the hollow above that perfect round ass. He sways and then lunges, bronzed and rippling arms lashing through the air.

"One two three step! Knees bent, you has to bend your knees!" he intones, scrambling the tenses in his charming Colombian accent. I try to follow him, try to match my own kicks and spread-eagle lunges to his frenetic pace, but it is all I can do not to faint from the heat.

Pablo is the salsa/Latin fusion cardio instructor at the exclusive and overly priced gym I joined four months ago during a free trial promo. This was in January, when everyone is full of resolutions. Mine was to lose twenty pounds, though I had already dropped thirty the preceding summer during a hellish breakup with Ben, my ex-fiancé. And then I saw Pablo. Needless to say, it was he who cemented my membership the moment he sprinted onstage during that first preview session. I haven't missed a Saturday morning class since—not that it has proven difficult. Since the breakup, I've gone on only three dates, all of them disastrous. And with zero prospects on the horizon, finding a healthy way to release the enormous energy reserves I carry from lack of sex seems paramount.

Sure, I use a vibrator—almost nightly, in fact. I'm a liberated woman, totally unashamed to own an online porn subscription and a drawer full of sex videos.

But it's not enough. And seeing Pablo every Saturday thrusting those hips in his loose, sexy running pants only magnifies it. I get wet looking at him. I know it's not just sweat, though anyone would be hard pressed to find a more demanding cardio class. Thanks in large part to Pablo, I did lose those twenty pounds, and for the first time ever I feel way confident about my body. So the irony of the fact that I am currently single and sexless is not lost.

So, here I was again on another beautiful, balmy Saturday morning. Today's class had been no different than usual; a brief warm-up followed by sixty achingly exquisite minutes of kinetically charged merengue and cumbia. As usual, I imagined Pablo dancing the samba naked in my apartment while I tried keeping up with his cha-cha-cha. Nothing new.

Sweaty and spent, I was already looking forward to showering and getting myself off at home as I exited the studio—so I was surprised when I felt a hand brush my lower back just before the door closed. I was shocked when I turned and saw Pablo.

Grinning, he extended his arms and beckoned me to do the same. Vaguely, I heard the opening riffs of a fast Cuban salsa. Ah, so he wanted to dance.

I looked around. A couple of ladies shot me envious glances as they left, but no one was watching otherwise.

Nervously I took his hands. They were firm and confident, used to leading. I hadn't salsa'd in nearly seven years; a dance- and fitness-phobe, Ben couldn't sway his hips to save his life. So I was surprised at how quickly we fell in sync, how quickly my body remembered the rhythms, like riding the proverbial bicycle.

"You're very good," said Pablo, even white teeth flashing in his chiseled brown face as he turned me, hips rotating at an impossibly obscene angle.

"Thanks," I responded, heart pounding. I tried not to fall in a puddle of mush at his feet. I felt dizzy from his scent, a blend of light cologne and man-smell. Silently I thanked myself for spritzing on a last-minute body spray this morning.

"I'm not surprised," he continued with his Spanish lilt, not missing a beat. "You always do so good in class."

This was the most we'd ever interacted. Pablo and I routinely exchanged smiles, had even once introduced ourselves when he helped me in the middle of class with a particularly challenging sequence. But now here he was before me, hips swiveling dangerously close to mine. I couldn't help but notice the faint outline of a sizable bulge through his pants. My nipples stood reflexively erect under my sports bra top. My panties were saturated.

The music stopped.

"*Gracias.*" Pablo whispered. "That was nice."

Graciously, slowly, he released me. Wordlessly I smiled and backed up to leave. I tried to appear confident, like I was the kind of woman used to dancing with hot Latin men every weekend. The studio was empty, though I could see a throng of people begining to crowd the hall, ostensibly waiting for our class to end. My running shoes scraped the floor as I half-walked, half-waded to the door. Once again, I felt his hand brush my back. Only this time it lingered.

"Christina," he said in Spanish, trilling the *r.* "Come."

Kickboxing was scheduled to begin in five minutes. Silently I followed him to the back of the studio and through an employee exit into an adjoining small room, one of the gym's private personal training spaces. The throng entered the studio as we stepped in. Windows flanking the front wall overlooked the now vacant hall.

Pablo closed the door and ushered me in, fingers lightly trailing my arm. Breathless, I shivered as he gently encircled my waist and drew me into his muscled chest. My face rested level with the hollow of his neck. I closed my eyes and inhaled his scent, which was like a warm forest, and then tilted my face, lips parted, to his.

Neither of us moved as his chocolate eyes seared mine, fire versus water.

His full mouth met mine. We kissed slowly, almost hesitantly, for a minute before something unleashed. My back arched involuntarily. My breasts pressed hard against his body, our tongues urgently and insistently intertwined. All shyness vanished as he half-led, half-pushed me to a small desk set against the back wall.

Quickly I sat on its surface, legs open, and breathed heavily as Pablo moved in between them, his cut body against mine. I felt his hard dick through his pants as he kissed me, and my pussy unloaded another torrent of moisture. I threw my head back, unable to stop shaking as Pablo trailed his fingers through my long hair. My headband fell to the floor, and my ponytail tumbled loose as he nibbled and then bit my neck, hot breath on my skin. His hands, used to leading, rubbed my hips and then traveled upward to my breasts, cupping and kneading them through my bra as my own fingers stroked the black curls resting on the back of his neck. They felt surprisingly silky.

I lifted my arms as Pablo removed my bra. My swollen and aching breasts came free as I clawed at his shirt until it fell away, revealing taut, broad pecs. He took one finger and lightly, slowly traced it around my nipple, smiling. Teasing. His pink lips curved upward, and for the first time I noticed how enviably long his eyelashes were. Tension built inside me to the point of bursting, to the point where I couldn't endure it, and I pulled his head into my breasts. He licked them greedily, sucking hard at my nipples, taking them gently between his teeth, alternating between one and the other. I shuddered and tugged at his waistband, hand brushing the dark hairy line extending downward from his navel. The fleshy tip of his head peeked out from his white briefs, radiating heat to the touch. I moaned, longing to suck it, longing to ram it inside me. It had been too long since I'd felt a real dick up my pussy, too long since I'd slurped on a rock-hard head. My other hand rubbed his steely asscheeks.

I couldn't stand it.

On the far side of the room lay a stack of red gym mats. With a heady exhalation I extricated myself from Pablo, legs and arms akimbo. I threw a mat on the floor and took off my shorts and dripping panties. I lay on the mat, elbows propped up, knees spread wide, offering up my snatch. I was thankful that I'd waxed.

"Take me," I said.

Pablo stood before me, eyes drinking me in, tongue flicking across his lips as he studied my vulva. Ever so s-l-o-w-l-y he hooked his thumbs in his pants and pulled them down along with his briefs. His long brown cock, uncircumcised, tilted erectly to the side, toward a slim hip. Those hips.

He knelt.

I expected him, wanted him, needed him, to enter me. Instead he cradled both of my knees and lay on his stomach, face inches from my pussy. I could smell myself, could smell the musky odor that meant I'd been too long without sex, too long without orgasm. I pinched my nipples, body aching to come.

Pablo buried his tongue between my pussy lips and then retreated. Agony. I saw a thin sticky line of glistening wetness, come, extend from my pussy to his mouth. He swallowed it and, exhaling, bent once more into my pussy. I felt him touch the tip of his tongue to my clit and I almost exploded. Again he retreated and looked up at me, brown eyes teasing, desire clouding them. One of his hands slid up to my breast, covering my fingers. Again he buried his face in my pussy, only this time with an intensity I had not yet seen. I couldn't help but moan as then, and only then, he began to really eat my pussy. His tongue lapped in between my lips, up and down, from the bottom near my ass to my engorged clit, over and over until I nearly came, gushing wetness into his mouth. I have always ejaculated, and always felt a little self-conscious about it as most men tend to freak out a little. But Pablo literally ate it up. I watched his head bob up and down, watched his face move side to side as he closed his eyes and fucked me with his tongue, hands now squeezing my asscheeks as I pumped my hips into his face, covering him with sticky sweet juice. Pablo burrowed harder, deeper, and placed my entire swollen pink clit firmly in his mouth, groaning all the while. More wetness. Clear liquid juices ran down his jaws onto my ass and onto the mat as he sucked and devoured my pussy.

That's when I closed my legs around his neck and, back arched to the ceiling, came in a series of waves. Wave after crushing tidal wave consumed me, overpoweringly relentless. Pablo's knuckles turned white as he held me down, holding my hips to the floor as he continued to eat my pussy while I came, sucking and slurping and swallowing, his tongue thrusting to my G-spot, nose buried in my thin racing strip of pubic hair. That's when I came again, harder and more powerful than before, into his open and waiting mouth.

I screamed and saw only blinding whiteness.

My fingers clutched at his hair. My legs felt like jelly.

I fell wholly on the map, gasping and panting as Pablo sat up. His face shone. He smiled.

"Is good?"

"God, yes," I managed to say, still breathless.

We remained that way momentarily, me quivering, him outlining the contours of my body with his strong, now sticky wet, hands. From the corner of my eye I saw his cock. It was still hard, a darkish and swollen blue-brown. Veins ran along the shaft and culminated at his reddish, throbbing head. Drops of white precome shone at the tip even as more oozed from his hole.

No way in hell were we finished.

In a flash I sat up and straddled him, one hand flanking the shaft, the other massaging the base. Pablo's coarse pubes were black and neatly trimmed. He grunted as I masturbated him, slowly at first, then with building speed. His hips, those hips that I'd spent four months ogling while he danced salsa, jerked rhythmically up and down with my hands. This time he lay on the slippery mat, writhing and staring at me as I hovered over his pelvis and jerked him off, my pussy centimeters from his cock.

I was still wet.

I took one hand and slipped it in my pussy as, still straddling him, I rubbed my clit. My other hand squeezed his massive balls.

Suddenly he stopped and rose.

I watched, frustrated, as Pablo crossed the room to his pants lying on the floor and retrieved a wallet. Quickly, expertly, he pulled out and put on a condom...a good thing, since I hadn't been on the pill in a very long time. I rubbed my clit harder, fully expecting him to rejoin me on the mat so that I could ride him to oblivion.

But he didn't. Instead I saw him enter the room's small storage closet and emerge with a giant blue medicine ball, the kind used in the gym's yoga classes.

Wordlessly he placed the ball in front of me and helped me stand.

Then he turned me around and bent me over the ball, then immediately spread my legs and entered me from behind.

Bliss.

We fucked for a long time. In, out, in, out, over and over, for what seemed like a beautiful eternity. His cock fit perfectly, filling me entirely and hitting my G-spot every time he thrust, balls slapping the back of my pussy. Wet slurps and sounds filled the hot room. My breasts bounced and jiggled, nipples hitting the blue rubber every time Pablo pulled me back toward him. His fingers dug into my asscheeks, burning and hurting but incredible.

At one point Pablo pulled my hair, throwing my head back. It was then that I noticed we were positioned directly in front of the room's main window. Somewhere in the distance I heard voices and the thumps of kickboxing in the adjoining studio.

Always shy, suddenly I didn't care.

"Pull it hard, baby. Please," I begged.

Pablo clutched my hair harder. I bucked against him, wet ass and pussy now completely enveloping his rock-hard cock as it rubbed my G-spot. I came again, harder than before. Wet trails fell from my pussy lips onto the base of his cock.

Finally he exploded. I felt Pablo jerk and then release. My stomach slid off the ball as he went momentarily limp. I felt heat through the condom and knew he'd come hard, too. Easily, languidly I moved my ass around, his cock still firmly lodged within me even as he slumped over my back, hands resting on my breasts. Slowly he released himself.

That's when we fell, exhausted, onto the soaked mat, panting heavily and sweating. Silence and the smell of sex hovered in the private training room. Dimly I heard more voices and foot-steps emanating from the studio. The kickboxing class was over.

Instead of getting up, I turned over to Pablo, now lying calmly on the mat beside me. He was glistening. Beautiful. He turned on his hip and faced me, gorgeous eyes searching mine. That's when I curled up in his arms, unmindful and uncaring of the fact that at any moment a throng of kickboxers, or at least one eager student seeking private training, might walk right by. I buried my head in his chest and inhaled his smell, my smell. I closed my eyes and sighed, spent from the best, most personalized workout I'd ever experienced.

SWITCH

Vanessa Vaughn

Dana pulled into the driveway slowly, her car's engine purring. Shifting into PARK, she grabbed her morning coffee mug from the cup holder and her briefcase from the backseat. She opened the door and stood for a moment, taking a deep breath and stretching her back. It had been a long day, but she was home now.

She saw two boys riding by on bicycles. "Hello, Mrs. Loper," they called.

She waved in their direction, smiling but exhausted. "Hello, boys."

Dana kicked the car door closed with a high heel, fumbling with her keys as she approached the front door. She pushed it open.

"Honey, I'm home," she cooed as she strode inside.

"In here, babe," came a muffled voice from the next room.

So he was already there. Good.

She sat down her briefcase and keys, picking up the mail by the front door. She sorted through a few envelopes and looked them over before kicking off her shoes and picking them up. In her stocking feet, she padded silently toward the bedroom, her heels dangling casually off of two fingers. She walked down the familiar hallway, and then opened the door. Michael looked in her direction as she entered. He stood at the closet, pulling off his tie. "How was your day?" he asked, hanging his tie up on the rack.

"Oh, fine," she said, walking toward him. "You?"

"The usual."

She leaned in for a quick kiss. He pulled off his shirt as she sat on the bed to remove her hose.

"You going to start dinner soon?" she asked. "I'm starving."

"I'm on it," he assured her, flashing his best smile.

Oh, she did love Fridays. She knew exactly what was coming. "Thank you," she said, standing. She put a hand to the side of his cheek and kissed him again.

She watched him pull on a pair of jeans that were a little tighter than usual. They had a slightly feminine cut to them, but he could get away with that. He was close to her size, lean and tall. As he pulled on a T-shirt, she watched his dark hair fall into place. God, he was good-looking.

He headed toward the hallway. "That's right, get in there and make me some dinner," she called, teasing him. She knew it would make him smile as he continued on his way to the kitchen.

Dana slid off the rest of her clothes and then stood in front of the closet naked, considering her choices. To the left were her usual selections—sundresses, tank tops, skirts—but those she ignored. To her right were her clothes for Friday nights. She eyed them for a moment, fingering the fabric. Then she chose a pair of dark slacks and a white collared shirt. She removed them from the hangers and laid them on the wide bed behind her.

She stepped back, closed the closet, and made her way to the dresser by the door. She opened her underwear drawer and glanced at the colorful lacy assortment. Then she reached far into the back. She brought out a white pair of men's briefs and tossed them on the bed.

She reached to the back of the drawer again. This time she brought out a clear harness, which she stepped into and pulled up onto her hips. She quickly adjusted the straps around her waist and on the very tops of her thighs.

She grabbed the briefs from the bed and stepped into them. As she slid them on, she stole a glance at herself in the long mirror on the wall. Just pulling these on made her feel sexier, more confident. She already felt entitled to act differently.

She put her hand into the drawer again and brought out a flesh-colored dildo. It was absolutely realistic looking, with small veins poking out on the sides and a beautiful fat head at the tip. She held it in her hands for a moment and stroked it with her fingertips. Just the shape of it turned her on.

Dana took the dildo and slid it inside her briefs. She couldn't fit it into the ring of the harness, because it would be at too extreme an angle under her clothes, a permanent erection. Instead, she adjusted it gently. Watching herself in the mirror, she angled it just right and removed her hand from her shorts.

She quickly stepped into the bathroom, then, grabbing a

role of elastic bandage, she returned to her previous spot in the bedroom. The bandage was made of a flexible, tan fabric. It was the kind usually used for wrapping sprained ankles or injured knees, but Dana planned to use it for something else. She lifted the fabric to her breasts. They were only average size, but she couldn't wear a bra under her shirt, and she didn't want her nipples to show through, either. She wound the bandage around herself several times before securing it and lowering her arms. She bound her breasts firmly, but not too tight, still giving herself a nice flat boyish chest.

She eyed her new body, striking a languid *contrapposto* pose in the mirror, her hand hovering near her package.

She was satisfied with the effect.

Dana turned back to the rest of her clothes. She pulled them on at once, tucking the white collared shirt into the slacks. The pants were loose, hiding the last of her feminine curves. She slid on a pair of socks and men's shoes from under her side of the bed.

Next, she went into the bathroom and stepped up to the mirror, looking closely at her hair. It was short enough, but blow-dried into a flowing feminine style. She brushed through it, pushing it more closely against the sides of her head, then grabbed a can of Michael's hairspray and fixed it into place.

Michael. The thought of him sent electric shivers up her spine. He was perfect, beautiful. She wanted him. Suddenly she felt possessive of him. She smiled. And he was in there right now fixing her dinner.

Dana unconsciously licked her lips as she walked to the hall. She moved with long, sure steps, a slight swagger underneath them. She moved like he usually did, as if he owned the place—which he did, of course, but then she owned it too.

She crossed the living room and entered the kitchen, greeting him casually. His eyes moved over her as she approached him. She knew how much she turned him on when she was like this, but was it her manliness or her attitude? He turned back to his cooking and she came up behind him and bent to kiss him on the cheek. It was clean shaven, baby smooth, and kissable.

She pushed her pelvis close to his perfectly rounded ass. She could feel his shape in those formfitting jeans; she also knew that he must be able to feel her. The dildo was at the front of her pants, rubbing up against him. He stopped for a moment. She knew he must be keenly aware of what he felt. She heard his breath catch in his throat.

They were roughly the same height, but he was barefoot right now. In these shoes, she was slightly taller. She put her arms around his waist and peered over his shoulder.

"So, what're we having?" she asked, breaking the spell.

"Oh, a little salad," he said, gesturing at the cucumbers and tomatoes he was cutting up. "Steak..."

"My favorite," she said into his ear. He popped a sweet tomato into her mouth. She bit it, feeling the juiciness explode onto her tongue as she punctured the thin skin.

"...and green beans," he said, lifting the lid of another pot to let the savory smell of the beans sautéing in chopped garlic and butter escape.

She took a step toward the pot, leaning over it to inhale the mouthwatering scent. "Heavenly," she said.

"It won't be long till it's ready," he said, stirring the pot.

She crossed the kitchen to the far side, opening a cabinet. She removed a glass tumbler and a bottle of scotch. She poured herself a few fingers and returned the bottle to the shelf. Dana grabbed the glass and carried it to the kitchen door.

"Just let me know, hon," she said with her back turned as she walked into the living room.

Dana grabbed the newspaper and sank into the comfortable leather chair. She reclined and sipped the oaky amber-colored liquor. It was her prerogative. After all, she had had a hard day at work, a hard week, in fact. Leaning back, she spread the paper open and crossed her legs, hooking her left ankle on top of her right knee the way Michael often did. She scanned the pages and continued to sip. In the other room, she could hear the pleasant soothing noises of a dinner being prepared for her. She could smell the sizzling steak and the garlic. Her mouth watered.

There wasn't much that interested her in the paper today, but that wasn't the point. The idea was for her to relax a little, to sit back and enjoy. She took another sip and closed her eyes for a moment, letting the liquid swirl around on her tongue. It tasted strong to her. She felt she was eating the fumes as she swallowed. It gently but pleasantly burned her throat on the way down.

Her thoughts wandered as she sat. She pictured the way she had looked standing in the mirror in the bedroom, her chest bound and boyish. She remembered the way she had felt standing there in her briefs, adjusting the dildo just so. Thinking about it made her wet. She brought her hand to her crotch in a protective gesture, cradling the bulge in her pants.

God, she wanted to fuck. But not just yet. She heard the sound of sizzling steaks being taken off the grill. The knobs clicked into place as the stovetop burners were turned off one by one.

Then she heard him calling softly. "Sweetie, it's ready," he announced. She heard the metallic sound of pans being laid in the sink.

"Coming."

Dana folded her newspaper and put it to the side. She downed the last swallow of her scotch and placed the glass on a side table. Clasping the wide leather armrests, she slowly raised herself to her feet.

In the kitchen, the food was already laid out for her. Two places were set at the table, food arranged perfectly on the round white plates. Extra helpings of everything waited in bowls in the center.

Dana gave him a warm smile. "Looks good enough to eat," she joked.

She sat at the table, giving him a minute to put the last of the pans in the sink.

At last he joined her. Michael approached the table, wiping his hands on a plain white apron he had worn to keep the grease off his clothes as he cooked the steaks. He stopped at his chair, untying the white strings behind him and sliding the apron over his head. He laid it on the counter and sat down.

Dana shook a little salt and pepper over her meat. She picked up her fork and steak knife and sliced into the tender cut. She bit into the triangle of steak, feeling the juices flow out. She could taste the dark grill marks with the top of her tongue. Dana complimented him. She looked back down at her plate and the glistening pink sliver cut into the thick cutlet. She thought again of her pussy and how wet she was. Her lips almost ached from how long she had been waiting.

As they talked, Dana looked him up and down hungrily. She reached out to rub his upper arm affectionately. They discussed her week at work, their plans for the weekend. Dana mentioned some chores she had to get done in the backyard.

Dana watched his fingers as he ate. She eyed the smooth pink cupid's-bow curve of his mouth. Just now, she thought of him as something more delicate than usual. She looked over his chest, imagining the way he looked beneath the T-shirt. She tried to picture not the muscles there, but just the small pink nipples. She felt a flickering in her clit and knew this was turning her on. She shifted in her chair, adjusting her pants a little.

After a few more bites, she leaned back, feeling full. Michael pushed the plate toward her playfully and reminded her to finish her vegetables. With a friendly but sarcastic roll of the eyes, she complied.

Finally, Michael sat back as well and laid down his fork. Dana was full too, but she knew she wasn't satisfied. She wondered how he felt. As they talked about the meal, Michael stood and collected the plates. He scraped the leavings into the garbage and set the white dishes into the sink with the pots and pans.

"Well, I guess I'm done here," he said, wiping his hands. "Your turn for the dishes."

"What?" Dana said, turning in his direction. "No, it's your turn this time."

"But after every time we switch," he said.

Dana rose from the chair and approached him. He looked delicious leaning there against the sink. "I know. So your turn," Dana insisted.

"I don't think so."

Michael took a step forward, but Dana caught him by his wrist. She brought her body behind him, pushing him against the counter. She leaned forward over him, holding his hands against the countertop.

She looked down at the perfect line of his lower back. She pushed her hips toward him, grinding into him as he arched back a little. She could feel his body against her, nervous but inviting. She knew he wanted it. He had wanted it all night.

"Well, maybe we could work out some kind of deal," she said.

They were both breathing harder. "Anything you say," he whispered.

Roughly, she reached around him, unbuttoning his jeans. She pulled them down and kicked them to the side. She could see the curve of his ass now, beautifully exposed in front of her. She was in complete control of him. He was hers for the taking.

She brought her arms to his hips, moving them slowly up the sides of his stomach and chest. She took in his heat, the touch and smell of him as she did this. She moved her hand up the back of his head, feeling the texture of his dark hair slide through her fingers. She closed her eyes.

Dana couldn't wait any longer. She reached for her fly, unzipped the front of her pants, and lowered them a little. Gently, she reached into her briefs and grabbed the dildo, fitting it through the ring of the harness. She lowered her briefs and looked down at it standing there, hard and firm. She stroked it a few times and imagined the sensation traveling through her.

She backed up a step.

"Now turn around and kneel down," she ordered.

Silently, looking down toward the floor, he turned and knelt in front of her.

"Now suck it," she said.

He reached up with one hand, touching the underside of her cock. He stroked the length of it and then brought his mouth to the tip. Looking submissively up at her, he took it in his mouth. He slid it in up to the hilt and then back.

She closed her eyes and leaned her head back with a groan. As he blew her, the base of the dildo pushed against her pussy, exciting her. He began to suck her faster and harder, the harness grinding against her. All the time, his eyes looked up, searching for her approval. She moaned.

"Oh, that's good," she purred. She could feel her blood quicken. He was so perfect, so sensual, kneeling there on the kitchen floor. She put a hand to the back of his head, guiding him roughly in and out.

He worked her as she pushed against the ring of the harness, getting wetter all the time. She was getting lightheaded. No, she couldn't end it like this. She wanted more. She gripped the back of his hair and pulled him away.

"Stand up," she commanded.

As he stood, she could see how hard he was. His dick stood at attention, ready to fuck her, but that she wouldn't allow. She pushed him backward against the countertop. He half-sat, half-stood at the edge, thrown slightly off balance. She grabbed his wrists and pinned them to his sides, leaning him back completely.

With one hand, she lifted the front of his shirt slowly, looking at his taut beautiful stomach. She raised it farther, just enough to reveal his small round nipples. Seen this way, they seemed more sexual than usual, like something hidden, something forbidden. She leaned over him, clamping her lips to one of them. She sucked it gently, flicking it with her tongue, then bit down hard and felt him squirm against the counter.

She raised her head and looked him in the eye. Opening her mouth, she brought the fingers of her right hand across her tongue, making them glistening and wet. Holding his gaze, she lowered her hand, moistening the tip of her erection.

He closed his eyes and stiffened. He knew what was next. Playfully, she sought out the puckered surface of his round hole and moved against it gently. Surely he could feel the slippery dildo teasing him. She could feel the fleshy opening ready to give way.

"Do you want it?" she asked.

"Yes," he whispered, still averting his eyes. The skin of his back and shoulders was pressed against the cold surface of the counter.

"You want me to fuck you?" she demanded, pushing firmly up against him. She watched his dick twitch eagerly as she said those words.

"Yes," he insisted.

With that, she leaned toward him and grabbed him by the hips, sliding into him.

As she did this, she felt a delicious pressure against her clit. She could hear his breath stop in his throat for a moment as the shock hit him. His muscles tensed.

She felt a power then, as if she owned him, as if he was incredibly vulnerable, there only for her pleasure. Was this how men felt when they fucked her?

She pushed into him again, harder this time. He gasped a little as she entered. His member rubbed against her belly with each thrust, getting harder all the time. She could tell he would come soon. She could tell that he loved it.

She pulled his hips to her and rode him then, driving her cock into him rhythmically. She could feel the pressure building against her pussy. She was wet and eager.

"Do you like that?" she demanded.

In answer, she felt his breathing change. He gripped her forearms and brought his head forward. His body spasmed against her gently.

Dana closed her eyes to savor the moment, her pussy throbbing impatiently beneath the harness. She cradled the back of his head as she felt his creamy wetness pumping onto his stomach. She felt him shudder. They stayed like that for several moments.

Eventually, she placed a hand on his thigh and slid out of him ever so slowly. She removed the dildo from the ring and tucked it back into her briefs. Michael stood, stepped in front of her, and took her roughly by the shoulders. He pressed against her, kissing her firmly on the mouth, their tongues working together. She could feel the wetness of his come now against her skin. Dana smiled and playfully swatted him on the ass.

She removed her stained shirt and leaned backward against the counter with an intense longing stare, her taut stomach now visible. Her delicate left hand rested in the sink, flicking the soapy water near the dishes.

"Your turn," she insisted.

GOOD PONY

Scarlett French

"Bend over," she said.

"I'm sorry?" I replied, rather taken aback.

"I said 'Bend over.'" Buki looked at me with impatience, a black riding crop poised in midair.

I looked again at her, then at the riding crop. Then I looked around the shop. None of the customers appeared to have noticed, but this was England, and people tend to be polite about such things.

"Ah, Buki, I don't think that it's in my job description to get assaulted by colleagues."

"Suit yourself. I just thought it was worth you experiencing the snap of a riding crop so you could better talk to customers about them. This is the first time we've had Hamlet's Horse Supplies products in, and they're the best crops money can buy—Pony Club approved 'n' all."

I paused. I hadn't worked at the sex shop very long and still wanted to make a good impression, show myself willing when it came to learning about things that might not appeal to me in particular. But I felt a bit out of my depth. It was true that I hadn't sold riding crops before, so I needed to learn about them, but I would have preferred to whack one against my own hand to get a feel for them. Surely customers who bought stuff like that knew what they wanted anyway?

"Umm, okay, I guess," I said unconvincingly. It was a little unorthodox, even for a sex shop, but I made Buki promise not to do it too hard.

The crop made a *swish* sound as it sailed through the air, followed by a crack as it landed on my ambivalent behind. "Ahhh!" I cried out, and involuntarily stood up straight to get my arse out of harm's way. "That hurt, Buki!"

"Sorry," she said, deadly serious. "I'll do the next one softer." I still wondered whether this was absolutely necessary. I also wondered what my partner would make of it when I told him. We'd agreed that when we weren't out together, flirting with other people was okay, even good for the soul, but the conversation had never stretched to, "So what about if someone offers to spank me?"

Nonetheless, I bent over again for Buki. I'm not sure why. I could have told her I'd just try it out on my arm or something—it wasn't as if the shop was an abusive environment by any stretch of the imagination.

The crop was quieter this time, and I didn't have the sound to anticipate when it would land. I jumped as it made contact. Even through my jeans it still stung for a second. But it wasn't so bad. Buki did it a couple more times and asked me how it felt. I told her it hurt a bit still and I didn't like that, but maybe she could just do it a couple more times, a little softer? A couple of customers had noticed by now and glanced over. I smiled at them. "Quality control," I said, by way of explanation.

"Quality control and staff training," said Buki.

At that I stood up. "All right, enough of that. You're so toppy, Buki."

"Oooh, you're up with the terminology!" she said. "Thinking of exploring S/M?"

"No, I just take my job seriously, so I've been doing some reading."

A customer approached and asked for advice on a vibrator, so Buki went over with her, while I picked a crop from the pile in the box and felt the wide leather loop at its end. The leather was firm yet supple and didn't seem as intimidating as when Buki had wielded it. The loop was held in place with an expertly knotted thread that wound up along the length of the crop with perfection, not a single thread overlapping. The woven leather handle was comfortable in my hand, almost molding to the shape of my closed palm. I flicked the crop about and heard the *swish* as it sliced through the air. It had give, though—its length bending then springing back as I flicked it.

That night I told Ben about it. He was interested, as he is about most things—and he didn't seem too put out about the spanking from Buki. "Do you want to get one of these riding crops, then?" he asked. "I'm happy to redden your arse if it turns you on."

"Oh, no, I don't think so," I said. "It's not really my thing. It hurt too much anyway."

"Okay, well, you can always change your mind. Remember, I'm more than happy to give it a try."

"Thanks, honey, that's really sweet." I kissed him on the lips. They tasted like the espresso he had been drinking. I kissed them some more. We fell back on the sofa, our mouths mingling, our hands in each other's hair. That's how it was with Ben—like a faucet that just needed the tiniest turn to come on full force. We fucked right there on the sofa.

As I sat on the train the following morning, I found my thoughts returning to the Hamlet's riding crops. When I got in to work I made a point of lingering with them, adjusting and readjusting the equestrian-themed display, setting the varnished papier-mâché horse's head just so on the shelf, changing the orientations of the soft grooming brushes that we'd also just gotten in. Lastly, I fanned the crops again to spread them evenly in the canister. The display looked perfect. I stared at it for a while, then retrieved a shiny all-black crop from the canister, just to hold it. It truly was beautiful workmanship. I finally replaced it and went to the counter when I saw there were customers. I thought about that crop all week. Sex with Ben was sweet but it certainly wasn't lacking. It was just...well, maybe he was right: I was changing my mind about that crop.

Finally, on my last shift before the weekend, I bought it. I'd watched over it all week to make sure we didn't sell it. How I could tell my favorite one apart from the other black ones, I'll never know. But I could tell it apart. Perhaps it was the particular winding of glossy thread around the shaft. Perhaps the particular feel of the leather on the handle. Perhaps the shiny perfect hide of the loop. I bought it when I was working with another woman, Anne. Anne was as discreet as Buki was in-yer-face; I knew she would respect my privacy. Anne wrapped it in gold tissue paper because it stuck out the top of the bag and I didn't want any funny looks on the train.

As I got in the door, I slowed my pace to a saunter and wiggled into the living room. Ben was on the sofa watching telly. He turned to greet me. "Hello!"

"Hello," I purred.

"What's in that bag you've got there?" he asked, a smile creeping across his face.

"I decided I'd like to try out that riding crop after all," I said as I pulled it out of the bag and tore the tissue paper off.

"Oh, what a beauty," said Ben as he got up and came over to take a look. "It looks like it's very good quality," he said as he ran his finger over the ridges of thread along the shaft.

"Ah, do you think you might be into this sort of thing?"

"Well, I don't know. But you have to appreciate the craftsmanship," he said, fingering the leather loop.

"Oh, I already have," I said, placing the crop fully in his hands, almost ceremonially, as an acolyte would a samurai sword.

He bowed slightly. "Madam, shall we retire upstairs?" I loved it when he got all upper-class on me. I immediately dropped my backpack on the floor and followed him up the stairs.

"Hmm, I think I'd like you to stand with your hands on the wall and your legs spread, like how a cop makes a suspect stand to get searched on one of those U.S. cop shows," Ben told me. I did as he suggested, his instructions sending a little thrill down my spine. The A-line skirt I was wearing allowed me to spread my legs without resistance. As I placed my palms to the wall, my head naturally fell forward a little and I stared at the ground. Ben asked me to lift my head. I heard him open a drawer, then I felt fabric fall against my face as he pulled a scarf tight across my eyes and knotted the silk at the back of my head. This was new for us—I'd never been blindfolded before, but I trusted Ben—and the gathering pool of wetness between my legs. At first he flicked the crop in the air—I could hear him behind me, assessing its structure. Then I heard a *thwack* that made me jump, as he gave a lash to what sounded like his palm. Then silence. I waited, the anticipation building.

Suddenly, I felt it. He dragged the crop over my arse from one side to the other, then finally stopped and lifted it away with a flick. I still feared pain so I was glad for the protection of my skirt. Next I felt the crop sliding up my inner thigh, dragging my skirt up with it. When it reached my pussy, Ben began to slowly seesaw the crop back and forth along the crotch of my underwear. With every forward stroke he curved it up a little so it hit the underside of my clit through the fabric, which was already damp with my excitement. Each time, my whole body juddered. He returned to dragging the crop across my arse, back and forth, with a flick away at each end. Then finally the crop came down. It didn't hurt. And my fear of pain was now transforming into an urgent need to feel it on my bare cheeks. Where Buki had struck too hard, Ben was proving his skill, and his restraint. I sensed that Ben was enjoying his role as much as I was mine. Oh, god, I wanted my undies down but I daren't break the spell by moving my palms from the wall. For the same reason, oddly, I also didn't speak. There was something otherworldly about this experience, and I couldn't risk shattering the strange mix of heightening desire and calm that was mingling inside me. I decided to sway my hips a little, egging him on without taunting.

"Stand still," he said, matter-of-factly. I froze, wanting him to command me again. I was surprised that I was thrilled by this as our relationship was based on equality—in and out of the bedroom. But I was beginning to perceive that we could play with one aspect without compromising the other. I hoped that Ben sensed this too and felt safe to command me again. I stayed precisely still, concentrating, barely breathing.

"Take your hands from the wall and pull down your skirt and knickers." Oh, he was getting the idea all right. I did what he told me to, glad to unzip the skirt and get rid of it along with my underwear.

"Good. Now, replace your palms on the wall." I placed them back carefully and braced myself against the wall. He didn't make me wait long. I heard the rush of wind as the crop sliced through the air. It landed hard on my bare arse, an assault on my senses. But rather than crying out in pain, I felt a breathy sigh escape my lips. I was braced now for pain, ready for it even. But instead, the crop now snaked up my inner thigh and brushed my pussy lips ever so lightly. I shuddered deeply; a mix of pleasure and the heightened awareness brought by the anticipation of pain. Next the crop fluttered across my bare arsecheeks. I clenched over and over again for the strike but the fluttering continued until I began to relax.

By the time it did come I didn't expect it, but Ben's surprisingly expert hand had brought it down just right on my hypersensitive skin, causing an intense sensation somewhere in between pleasure and pain. But I wanted it now, wanted more. I could feel my arse swaying and arching of its own accord, goading Ben to strike me harder. My pussy was hot and wet and throbbing. I could feel it responding more and more, like an interpreter, translating the crop ministrations into a series of pleasures that seared through my core. Ben sensed it too and stepped up his efforts, landing the crop hard again and again, though never in the same spot, until I felt sure that my cheeks must be on fire.

"Oh," I cried out. "Fuck me. Please, Ben, fuck me! Get your cock in me now, please." I was desperate for him, driven mad with desire.

"You asked for it," he breathed as I heard his zipper go down and his jeans fall to the floor. I kept my palms against the wall but swayed my body in sheer need until I felt him grab my arse with both hands, his own palms cool against my stinging flesh. I felt his hard cock nudging between my arsecheeks. He had lubed up and his cock slipped against my perineum as it slid into my pussy. It felt like heaven. Every stroke sent waves of intense pleasure through me. And still I kept my palms on the wall. He fucked me slowly and rhythmically until I began to moan and pant.

"Mmm," he whispered in between sighs. "How about a little something gentle in your arse?"

At that suggestion, I felt my arsehole twitch in response. "Oh, yes, oh, god yes!" We hadn't had a lot of anal sex, but when we did Ben always worked me up very hot beforehand and so it always felt good. I had a feeling this was going to be the best yet. I felt him slip out of my pussy and reposition his cock, rubbing it back and forth against my already slippery perineum and arsehole. I could feel it puckering up to invite him in because I was so ready for it. He pushed the head of his cock in ever so slowly, and I gasped as I felt it slide past the first ring of muscle. He waited, then eased the length of his cock in. We both paused then as my arsehole adjusted to accommodate him. He reached his hand around and stroked my clit, and I felt myself open up even more for him. Finally, he began to slowly thrust, his cock sliding deeply inside my tight little arsehole. I cried out with the intense pleasure. I was so aroused that I could feel every tiny motion, every twitch of his cock. I even thought that I could feel his precome welling inside my arse, lubing it all the more, adding to the slipping and sliding within the delicious snugness of our fucking. Every thrust brought us both closer and closer until finally he said, "I'm going to come soon, baby. Where are you?"

"I'm almost there," I cried, my breathing ragged. "I just need..." I didn't finish the sentence. I wrenched one hand from the wall and put my fingers to work on my clit, stroking it hard and rhythmically while Ben's dick thrust in and out of my arsehole. My hips began to buck, pulling forward then slamming back onto Ben's cock until I heard, "Uh, I'm coming, I'm coming." As I felt him spasm against me, my own orgasm burst through me, from deep in my core to the top of my head and tips of my toes. We rocked together and sighed until our bodies slowed.

A couple of weeks later, we whiled away a Saturday wandering around the street markets of London's Brick Lane. In addition to registered stalls, sellers lined the streets, their wares on blankets laid out on the pavement. It was a great place to find bargains and curiosities. As we neared an antique stall down a particularly narrow street, I spotted something on a table, alongside a pile of beaten bowler hats and old suitcases. Ben followed quizzically until he saw what I had found. Amongst them sat an old leather riding saddle; a heavy, quality horse's saddle with tool work along its edges. Ben and I looked at each other and smiles crept across our faces.

"Ah, how much for the saddle?" I called out to the stall-holder. A portly middle-aged East End geezer, he surveyed us before answering. "Seventy-five quid," he said. He looked over at his mate and laughed as though he was wondering what a couple of city people were going to do with a saddle. His friend called out, "We'll bring you the horse next week!" They chuckled to each other, pleased with their joke.

"Oh, it's okay," smiled Ben. "I've already got a pony."

LUCKY

Xan West

I need to be forced to name my desires. I need to look them in the eye and accept them for mine. I need to travel that long journey through shame into pride. I am lucky to have someone willing to give that to me, who can go to those scary places with me. I am lucky to have Sir.

Sir knows me. Knows what I want. Knows where the edges are, and how to take me there. We go for intensity, and it is glorious, and scary, and cathartic. It would not work between strangers. It would not work if Sir didn't communicate my worth (and her love for me) in small daily ways.

At the leather conference, Sir dressed me in the morning. I knelt and she wrapped my wrists in cuffs. She had me wiggle into a garter belt and then sit on the bed, as she slowly rolled fishnet stockings up my legs and attached the garters, her fingers teasing my thighs. She pulled me to my feet, produced a skirt, and slid it up my legs, smiling with satisfaction when it barely covered my ass, leaving just enough bare thigh to show off the garters.

She removed the A-line shirt she had worn the day before and through the night, and slipped it over my head, tugging it down my large frame. It smelled like her, of sweat and cologne and that musky scent that is Sir. She pulled out a deep red lipstick, painted my lips with it carefully, then smiled wickedly and wrote something in lipstick on the shirt. She handed me my Frye boots and ordered me to polish them and put them on. She was in and out of the shower before I was done, and pulling on her socks just as I finished. Her boots were gleaming, polished first thing that morning, and I helped her into them, my eyes lingering on the sight.

She unzipped her fly and pulled out her cock, saying huskily "C'mere, slut," as she grabbed me by the hair and thrust my mouth onto her cock. I shuddered, feeling her deep in my throat, her hands fisted in my hair, fucking my mouth. She reached into me and named that core truth I rail against. I am a slut. I was helpless to ignore it with her dick in my mouth, and that was the point. I spend so much time resisting my own desire; these moments are when I can surrender to it, because she loves it, because it is safe, because I ache to so badly.

"That's my slut. I know how much you love getting your mouth fucked by me. This is who you are, slut. A hole aching to be fucked."

She thrust into my mouth quickly, grunting her pleasure, and then yanked me off her dick by the hair.

"Plant yourself on my boot, slut. Get it nice and wet."

My eyes lifted and begged her not to make me do this.

"Get to it, slut," she said gruffly, no mercy in her eyes.

I spread my legs and wrapped them around her boot, my cunt spasming as it contacted the leather. I was so ashamed that this turned me on. And so grateful that she made me face it.

"Ride that boot for me."

I thrust onto her boot, tears forming, pleading whimpers sliding out of my mouth.

"That's my good slut. That's it, ride out your pleasure on my boot. Don't stop riding it, baby. Open your eyes, let me see. You love this, don't you? I can see it in your eyes. You love being my good little boot slut. You can't stop until you come for me. I want your come on my boot all day, just waiting for your tongue to lick it up tonight."

Incoherent begging sounds emerged from my throat as I rode her boot. I knew the rules but I couldn't form the words. I couldn't stop fighting this. I battle in my head, every time. That's the point.

"That's my good slut. You love fucking yourself on my boot, don't you? I can smell you, slut. All day I'm going to smell you on my boot, and know you are mine."

My clit jolted, my cunt ached to be filled. Tears rolled down my face. I was ashamed and aroused and so fucking helpless. There was only one way to end this.

"Please, Sir. Please may I come for you, Sir?"

"I need you to say it, slut. Tell me you are my slut, and you may come."

I could feel my eyes get huge. There was a lump in my throat. She gripped me by the hair tightly and her voice was ferocious as she said over my whimpers, "Tell me. Tell me who you are."

"I am your slut," I whispered, and her hands released me as I came for her, writhing on her boot, tears rolling down my face, my cunt throbbing. There is no release like tears and orgasm combined, and she doesn't forget that. She lifted me to my knees and gently licked the tears from my cheeks.

"Look at yourself," she said warmly, lifting and turning me to face the mirror. My eyes were wide, face flushed, hair wild. My lipstick showed I'd been sucking cock. The A-line shirt was stretched out over my large tits and belly, so thin you could see my nipples clearly, and SLUT was written across my chest in red. My skirt had ridden up and my cunt peeked out, glistening. The fishnets had ripped, and the tough boots made me look decidedly queer. She had marked me, her scent enveloping me, her name for me emblazoned on my chest, her cock still on my lips. I am not just a slut, I am her slut, and her actions crystallized that fact. Being her slut makes me powerful.

She tugged my skirt down slightly and stood behind me, pulling the lock out of her pocket and locking my cuffs together behind my back. I stood tall and followed her out of the room, strutting, my shoulders back, my boots loud, my head high. I was proud to be seen with her, my handsome butch in leather.

All day she showed me off. The attention made me dizzy. A tall gorgeous man with chocolate brown skin, broad shoulders, predatory eyes, and fangs peeking out from his wicked smile admired my tits and growled in my ear, making my cunt spasm. A gorgeous Asian femme dyke eyed my legs as she talked to Sir quietly. Her boy, a short, square-framed Latina butch licked her lips and winked at me. Sir kept a hand on me all day, tugging my arms back by the cuffs to push my tits out farther, stroking the back of my neck, resting her boot on my thigh as I sat at her feet. Her touch casually claimed me, keeping my arousal high.

Late in the day, she brought me over to watch a pale redheaded trans boy black the boots of a gorgeous bear of a man with pale skin covered in gray fur. She unclipped my wrists, massaged my arms, and locked them together in front of me, sitting me down to watch as she approached the bear to whisper in his ear. He nodded, gesturing to the boy, and they continued to talk, the bear's eyes grazing my mouth, my thighs, my boots. I was mesmerized by them, watching the boy's hands work, and when he lay on his belly to lick the bear's boots, my cunt jolted and my breathing stopped. Sir returned to stand behind me, leaning in to my ear as she pinched my nipples.

"Come," she growled.

I did, trying to be quiet, my eyes locked on the boy tonguing those boots as I writhed in my chair.

"That's my good slut," she said. "I'm going to enjoy giving you away tonight."

My eyes widened. I imagined being given to the bear in front of me, my ass pounded by his cock. Or maybe his boy, using those strong hands to open me up. I could almost feel the vampiric man sinking his teeth into me as he rammed me with his cock. I could see that femme top holding me down for her boy, her nails raking my skin as her boy fisted me. I writhed in the chair, my cunt throbbing. I was trembling, my mind racing from one image to the next, until they all blended together and I met Sir's eyes, whimpering.

"Yes, slut. I'm going to offer you around. I'm going to make sure everyone knows how much you need to be fucked. You will be displayed for all to see. Everyone will know what a slut you are."

I was going to be displayed, naked in my desire. I shuddered, lowering my gaze. My clit was pulsing, my skin hot and flushed with shame.

Fear built through dinner. She sat next to me at a crowded table as I awkwardly attempted to eat with my wrists locked together, watching my face as I thought about saying no, calling it off. I was not sure I could do it. I barely tasted the food, and sat quietly as the table ordered coffee, my hands resting in my lap. Sir leaned over and whispered in my ear.

"Stroke your clit for me, slut. You may come as many times as you like, just do not make a sound."

I could feel the blush begin, heat racing up my skin as I reached for my clit under the table. I was sure everyone could hear the rings on my cuffs moving as I stroked myself. I gritted my teeth as I came and could feel tears form as I continued to stroke helplessly. I came two more times before coffee had been drunk, and she told me to stop, dinner was over.

I was so hungry to be fucked I would have gladly bent over in the lobby just to feel something inside me. Sir took me to the public playspace and detached my cuffs so she could put me in the sling. She clipped the cuffs to the sling and there I was, exposed. My skirt had ridden up, and I was spread wide, aching to be plundered. I felt so empty. She stepped back to look at me and shook her head, pulling out her pocket knife. She cut off the shirt, exposing my tits and belly, then stepped back. It still wasn't right. She pulled out that very same lipstick and wrote across my broad belly. I couldn't see it, and I was stuck in place, with no way to maneuver myself so I could read it.

She pulled her belt from her pants and stepped back, laying sting in waves along my upper thighs. She tapped my cunt with the belt and I yelped. Sir reached for something from her bag, fumbling with it, then placed it at the mouth of my cunt.

"Please, Sir," I whimpered.

"My slut wants to get fucked, mmm? Not just yet. Don't you want to know what's written across that gorgeous big belly of yours?"

I nodded.

"It says I AM A SLUT. PLEASE FUCK ME. That's what you need, isn't it? To be fucked. By me, by my friends. That's what you love, to be spread wide and fucked. Say it for me, and I'll fuck you, slut."

She teased around my opening as she talked. I was holding my breath. She had actually done it. The fantasy I'd had for years. It was going to happen that night. I couldn't believe she had done it. She pinched my nipple, jolting me out of my reverie.

"I won't fuck you 'til you say it, slut."

"Please, Sir. I am a slut. Please fuck me, Sir. I am your slut. Please, Sir. I need to get fucked. Please fuck your slut."

The baton slid in. It was cold and excruciatingly hard. My cunt contracted around it, and it was so unforgivingly, amazingly hard. So hard it ached. Once it was in deep, she kept it still.

"You don't even need a dick or a hand to come around, do you, slut? You'd come around anything as long as it was hard and deep, wouldn't you? All right then, slut. You may come as much as you want tonight, as long as you make it loud."

"Oh, god, Sir," I moaned as I came. "It's so hard, Sir."

"Yes it is, slut. That's right. And it's just the beginning."

She thrust it into me, and I came again, screaming for her, and it was still there, relentless, so intense that I began to cry.

"That's my slut. Cry for me. That's my good slut. Look up and see."

I did. There he was, the sexy man I had seen earlier with the vampire teeth. He growled in my ear and I came again, moaning. He had metal claws on his fingers and they traced over my skin. My eyes locked on his as he played me with them, watching me tremble. The baton slid out of my cunt and I whimpered as he moved toward my feet. His claws traced my thighs, ripped my fishnets; my cunt was spasming, empty. Sir was at my ear, her hand stroking my hair.

"Tell him," she said.

I couldn't. I shook my head, my eyes closed, trembling at the sensations his claws were invoking. His teeth sunk into my thigh, and I came, screaming.

"Tell him, or he won't fuck you," she said.

I choked on shame as I met his eyes. They looked even more predatory. I felt so naked. I took a deep breath. He took out his cock, and it was beautiful. He put on a condom. I could do this.

"I am a slut. Please fuck me," I said softly.

He rammed into me. His cock was large and pulsing and so alive. My cunt clamped down and he groaned in response. He bent over and drove his teeth into my neck as he shoved into me. I was coming in waves, it was one big circuit between his teeth and my cunt, building bigger and bigger. He lifted up and glided his teeth down to worry my nipple. I came hard, milking him as he growled. It went on forever it seemed until he raised his head and slipped out of me.

He moved to stand on my side next to Sir, and I felt a slick finger teasing my ass. I looked up and the bear was grinning at me. He was sliding fingers full of lube into me and stretching my ass with two fingers.

"Are you going to say it for me, hmm?" he said, his voice lilting. "Are you an ass slut? I bet you are."

He winked at me as his delicious fingers enticed me. I could see his boy stroking him, keeping his dick hard. It suddenly didn't seem so serious. I looked up at Sir and she was smiling. The butch-femme couple approached, big grins on their faces. I was surrounded by smiling people, all delighted at the opportunity to fuck me. A weight lifted and the words came easily.

"I am an ass slut. Please fuck me," I said.

"I thought you might be," he quipped, and they all chuckled.

He gripped my hips and eased into my ass. He felt amazing. The vampire leaned in and nipped at my neck. The femme stroked my thigh as her boy took my nipple in her mouth. The bear's boy fondled my other thigh. Sir leaned in and kissed me. I was surrounded by joy as I came. It rippled through me as the bear fucked my ass, and I could feel it gather in my stomach as it ramped up. He pulled out and gestured to his boy, as he moved up, taking off the condom and putting on a fresh one that smelled like mint. He slipped into my mouth at the same moment his boy entered my ass. He held my head still, and they fucked me together. I came, screaming and gagging around his cock as it rammed into my throat. My nipples were pinched, hands stroked my skin. I was covered in sex, dripping with it, on display for all. I joyously thrust back against the cock reaming my ass. I felt so lucky. The orgasm washed over me as it built and built and I began to fly, weightless, soaring on pleasure.

The bear pulled out of my mouth, and I could feel myself

begin to laugh as my cunt closed on air and my ass clamped down on his boy's dick. I was surrounded by laughter; we were all laughing as we fucked and kissed and stroked. Everyone was touching, and I was the conduit for all that energy, all that connection. Across gender, across orientation, we were sharing pleasure and joy and love.

"I am a slut! Please fuck me!" I shouted gladly for the whole room to hear as the bear's boy slipped out of my ass.

The femme pulled off her nails and slid on a glove, lubing it up. She stroked the edges of my cunt, teasing me with a grin, and then pushed three fingers right in. She leaned in and blew air right onto my clit, smiling as she felt me contract around her fingers. Her thumb reached up to stroke me and I came right there, moaning loudly.

"Yes!" I yelled.

She eased four fingers in, no problem now. That insistent rubbing built, concentrating in my sternum, as she twisted her fingers, spreading them. She tucked her thumb in, working with me to slide her whole hand into my cunt. Her boy stroked my clit as she entered me. My breath stopped. I held Sir's eyes and melted into them, feeling the energy whirl between my breasts. She was reaching right into me, and it felt like Sir reached down to hold her hand inside me, right there at my sternum.

Sir smiled, and said, "That's my good slut."

I came, grabbing that fist, screaming, tears streaming out of my eyes and into my ears. Hands held me, I was cradled and safe and so so full. I looked up and the femme was kissing her boy. The vampire was smiling at me and stroking his cock. The trans boy was licking the bear's nipples. Sir smiled proudly down at me and said, "I am so lucky to have you as my slut."

Her hand began to move inside me, and the intensity grew in my chest. I could feel her pulsing, moving so big inside me. It was suddenly too much, and my leg started cramping. She eased out and I was taken down slowly, allowed to stretch. They took me to a nearby futon. The femme's boy was sitting there, her cock out, waiting. They seated me upon it, facing the room. She was packing a long thick dick and it reached into me, pressing insistently against my cervix as I squirmed on it. Her hands reached around to pinch my nipples, and her mouth licked and bit at my neck. I writhed on her dick. It was so long, so relentlessly there. My muscles were exhausted, I was too tired to lift up, just stuck there, impaled on her cock.

Sir pulled out her dick and teased my mouth. I wanted her inside me more than anything.

"Say it for me," she said.

"Please fuck me, Sir. I am your slut, Sir. Oh, god please, Sir. Please fuck my mouth, Sir. I'm your cocksucking slut, Sir. Please, Sir. I am your slut, Sir."

She slapped my cheek with her cock.

"Tell me that again."

"I am your slut, Sir."

"Tell me that you are proud to be my slut," she insisted.

I came, riding the boy's cock, squirming, moaning. Her hands lifted my hips, thrusting me onto her, moving me as she growled.

"I am proud to be your slut, Sir. Please fuck your slut, Sir," I moaned.

Sir grabbed me by the hair and rammed her cock into my mouth. I gagged, and she kept fucking me, smiling down at me, telling me to choke on her cock. Helpless, I was filled, my mouth moved by Sir for her pleasure, the boy moving my cunt to please herself. I flew higher, holes filled, senses overwhelmed, proud to be exactly who I am. Her slut.

Later, my mouth on her boot, belly on the floor, surrounded and stroked by those who had helped her fuck me, I tasted my own come on the leather and was certain that I had gotten exactly what I asked for, precisely what I wanted. I lifted my head and smiled up at her.

"That's my good slut," she said gruffly, and stroked my cheek.

I am so lucky to be hers.

DESCRIBE IT

Lux Zakari

"God, I love your cunt," James half-sighed, his breath hot against Lisa's inner thigh.

Lisa smiled and raised her head up from the pillow. "Is that so?" she asked through a lazy yawn.

"Yes." He gave her clit a bold kiss for emphasis.

She squirmed with pleasure at the feel of his full lips. "And what's so great about it?"

"What isn't?" He rested his unshaven cheek against the inside of her leg and brushed a finger against her sex, which was still damp from their earlier lovemaking.

"I don't see what's so special about my cunt." She propped her arms up behind her head and neck for a better view of James's head of dark curly hair between her legs. She stifled a moan at the sight. “I mean, you’ve had other girls. You’ve seen other cunts.”

“So what? I like yours.” Again, he kissed her clit, this time giving it a flick with his tongue that was so quick Lisa thought she had imagined it. “It’s always been so good to me.”

She fell back against the pillow again. “I guess I just don’t see it the way you do.”

“I guess not,” James said softly. His smoldering eyes had a faraway look in them as he watched his finger move over her clit.

Lisa’s eyes squeezed shut and she took a deep breath, focusing on the sensations that his hand was eliciting. “So describe it to me,” she urged. “I want you to make me love my cunt as much as you do.”

An impish grin appeared on his face. “All right.” He traced the outer lips of her pussy with his finger, then his tongue. “For starters, your cunt reminds me of a rose about to bloom.”

“Don’t insult me with clichés,” she moaned, her hips twitching at his touch.

“Don’t worry, I’m just getting started. But it’s still true,” he chuckled, glancing up at her. A surge of passion rushed through him as he observed Lisa, gloriously naked in his unmade bed. Her olive skin glowed in the dim, gold lamplight, and her eyes remained closed as she gripped the pillow beneath her head in anticipation.

He lowered his head between her legs, splayed open just for him, and studied her. “Let’s see. What can I tell you that you don’t already know?” He used two gentle fingers in the shape of a *V* to spread her outer lips. “Well, for one thing, I see a spot you forgot to shave.”

“Where?” Her eyes fluttered open.

"Right here." His tongue lapped at a few sparse coarse hairs hidden in her folds.

"Never mind." Lisa attempted to close her legs with a groan of annoyance. "This is stupid. I'm embarrassed now."

"No, don't be." James clamped his hands on both of her legs and pried them wide open again. "You shouldn't care. I don't care. Don't you think that I love that you make the effort to shave for me?" He kissed her smooth mound. "It's unbelievably sexy."

She smiled despite her onslaught of shyness. "It isn't."

"Yes, it is." His kisses moved lower, over her sex, until he heard Lisa let out a sigh of both relaxation and bliss. "And I think it's sexy how swollen and red your clit gets when you're turned on. Like now."

"I'm not turned on," she said, her voice barely a whisper as she raised her pelvis to meet his mouth.

"I think you are." He slid one finger inside her, causing her to gasp. When he withdrew it, he added, "And it looks like you're very wet, too." He pushed his finger inside her again. "Your body never lies to me."

James bowed his head so his tongue could search out and circle her clit. Lisa moaned as his finger continued to dip inside her hot wetness, and her hips rose to meet his hand's motions.

"I love everything about your cunt," he murmured against her pussy. "I love the smell of it—like the beach mixed with vanilla."

"It's just the lotion I use," she gasped out, her words strained, her cheeks flushed, and her honey-colored hair tangled and spread out across the span of the pillow.

"It's you," he told her. His tongue swept across her clit like a wave just as he added another finger inside her dripping pussy, eliciting another strangled cry from Lisa. "I love how wet your cunt gets for me, and how tight it gets when you get close. I can tell you're close right now."

"I am," she whimpered, her breasts rising and falling with every sharp intake of breath she took. She reached down and tangled her fingers in his unruly hair. "So shut up already and get down to it."

James bit back a smile and obeyed her request. Her thighs warmed his cheeks and his ears as his tongue and lips moved rhythmically over her clit and his fingers continued to plunge inside her, bringing her swiftly to orgasm. Her fingernails scratched against his scalp as shudders wracked her body and she cried out his name.

He kissed his way back up her body while she lay frozen to the mattress, still whimpering quietly, her body tingling. His mouth found hers and she kissed him back with as much energy as she could muster and with all the feeling she had bubbling inside her like champagne.

"So what do you think?" James asked, nuzzling her neck. "Did I change your mind?"

"I'm not sure," Lisa said softly as she turned to face him, a smile spreading across her heart-shaped face. "I might need more convincing."

WAITING FOR THE RIVER

Kris Adams

They'd never really spoken before, so Fanny was surprised when Wanda invited her to lunch on the last day of her six-month temp assignment. She was even more surprised when the other woman mentioned a favor she wanted to ask.

Wanda ate quickly, nervously. Fanny tried to be patient, but her curiosity was piqued, and the lunch hour was quickly coming to a close.

"Are you going to ask me this favor yet?" Wanda looked up with panicked eyes. "We have to get back to work, and you seem so nervous about this. Just ask me."

"I'm sorry. You're right." Wanda lowered her fork and cleared her throat. "Okay, um. I remember hearing you say that you have a digital camcorder, right? Well, Marc, my boyfriend, he's in sales, so he travels a lot." She played with a loose tendril of dark hair. "Sometimes I don't see him for weeks on end. And it's hard—for him. To not see me." Wanda's eyes pleaded for understanding. "You know?"

"Sure."

Wanda continued, more softly and more slowly than before. "So I—I mean, we—were thinking, maybe I should make a video. For him. When he's on the road. That he could watch." She looked up and whispered, "A personal video."

"A personal vi—ooooh." Fanny sat back in her seat and grinned at Wanda's jumpiness. "You want to borrow my camcorder and make a home se—"

"Sssssshhhhh!" Wanda hissed as she covered her eyes and scrunched down in her seat. "Don't say it out loud!"

Fanny would have rolled her eyes at her coworker's paranoia...if she hadn't thought the paranoia was kind of cute. "People do it all the time. I can bring it in tomorrow. Do you and Marc need the tripod?"

"Um." If Wanda could have looked even more mortified than before, she did just then. "No, I...that's not what I meant." Elbows on the table between them, Wanda hid her face in the back of her hands, leaned forward, and muttered, "I was wondering if...if youcouldtapemebymyself." She kept her eyes squeezed shut in preparation for a crushing blow, but it didn't come.

"Um. Yeah, okay, why not?"

Wanda pulled back quickly and sank down into the booth. "Okay. Thanks," she replied under her breath, just as the waitress came to drop off the check. "Lunch is on me." She bit her lip and looked at Fanny with doe eyes. "I feel like I should buy you dinner, too."

"Yeah," Fanny whispered. "You probably should."

Fanny smiled and tried not to look at her watch. Once they'd arrived at the hotel room and Wanda had quickly slipped into the bed, they'd made pleasant if awkward small talk for nearly ten minutes. Fanny decided she needed to get things moving. "Is there anything you need me to do to make you more comfortable? More wine?" Wanda bit her lip and then her eyes darted quickly over to her purse. Fanny slid out of her chair and retrieved Wanda's handbag. Wanda took out a DVD.

"It's Marc's," she muttered as she handed the disc to Fanny. "Not that I'm into watching that stuff or anything!"

"Of course not." Fanny smiled as she turned on the television and put in the blank DVD. There were no ads, no menus, no chapter selections, just a scene of a woman asleep in a bed in a dark-lit room.

"I just grabbed one of my boyfriend's DVDs. They all look the same to me," she explained, badly. "I just thought that I might be too nervous without some, um, visuals."

"Whatever you want." Fanny returned to the chair next to the camera and located her subject through the viewfinder. "Whenever you're ready." Wanda fidgeted on the bed like she couldn't get comfortable. She let out a deep breath and fixed her gaze on the television screen, where the sleeping woman was slowly coming awake. After five minutes she'd only progressed to gently rubbing her hands over her chest. Fanny made a small yawn. "How long have you been with your boyfriend?"

"Eighteen months. He's a good guy. I mean, as good as one could expect."

Fanny nodded. "You two have a good time together? I mean, you know, you enjoy yourselves, right?"

"Oh, sure." Wanda smirked. "He's very sexual. He wants me all the time."

"Sure he wants you...but does he get you off?"

"Well, um. He doesn't...I don't always...um...with him."

"So not so much with him. But you can by yourself?"

"Mostly."

"Go on."

Wanda smiled proudly. "Sometimes, when he's away, he'll call me late at night and we have...you know...on the phone." Fanny nodded and discreetly pressed the record button on the remote control for the camera. "Have you ever done that?"

"Have I ever had phone sex? No, I can't say I have."

A pleased look crossed Wanda's face. "Really? I'm surprised."

"Why?"

"Well, I just thought that you'd have done a lot...because you're—"

"Because I'm what?"

"Oh...I just thought that you were...um." Wanda blushed and stretched her legs out. "I mean, I've never heard you talk about a guy or anything," she explained, eyes on the floor.

"Well, if that's the case, wouldn't you be more comfortable with someone else doing this—in case I try to hit on you?" Fanny snapped.

"I'm sorry. I don't care. I just couldn't ask any of my girlfriends at work to do this, and since you're leaving—"

"You'll never have to look me in the face after tonight, right?"

"Sorry."

"Whatever. You were saying—"

"So, are you?"

"I thought you said it didn't matter."

"Just curious." Fanny said nothing, then Wanda added quickly, "Why did you agree to this anyway? It's a strange request, especially since we won't be seeing each other anymore."

"Maybe because we won't be seeing each other anymore." Fanny stared at her knees silently until she was distracted by the panting coming from the television. The woman on the screen was tugging on her panties. When Fanny looked up she was unnerved by Wanda's rapacious glare. She took a deep breath and watched Wanda mirror her. "Wanda. Why don't you tell me a fantasy."

"All right."

Fanny knew she was on the right track, but her patience started to wear thin five minutes into another massage-and-bubble-bath story. Wanda hadn't made much progress. And her eyes were glued to the woman rubbing herself through her panties on the screen. Both were moving too slow for Fanny.

"Let's try something else." Fanny motioned for Wanda to lie flat on her back. "Close your eyes."

"What's that?"

"It's just a blindfold, don't worry." The thin black silk scarf had been the last thing she'd grabbed on her way to the hotel, but something told her she might need it. Once she'd tied it firmly around Wanda's eyes, she checked the battery on the camera and turned the volume up on the TV. "Now. I want you to pretend that you're her, the woman on the screen." Wanda nodded but only shifted underneath the covers. Fanny checked the battery again; one bar had already disappeared. "Lick your lips for me, okay? Now. I want you to pull down the bedspread for me."

A faint, "Okay," slipped from Wanda's lips as she slowly pushed the thick bedspread down to her knees, leaving the flat sheet to cover her up to her collarbone.

"Now, tell me what you'd want your boyfriend to do to you right now."

"I don't—"

"You do know, you just have to say it."

Wanda took a deep breath. "Well, I guess I'd like for him to touch my face. My mouth."

"How?"

"Softly."

"Show me. Pretend that your hand is your boyfriend." There was a slight nod, and then Wanda's fingers inched toward her mouth. They trembled slightly as they traced her lips. "Wet your lips again." This time Wanda made a small, barely audible moan when her tongue made contact with her fingers. She suckled them without being told. "That's good," Fanny whispered. "Do you like to suck your boyfriend's fingers? If your boyfriend were here, would he...slide his tongue deep inside your mouth?" When Wanda nodded quickly, Fanny added, "Are you thinking about your boyfriend right now?"

"Uh-uh," Wanda replied around her licked wet fingers.

Fanny waited until Wanda's hand started sliding toward her breast. "Are you thinking about the woman in the movie?" Wanda didn't answer, but both hands cupping her breasts through the sheet was answer enough. "Are you picturing her?"

"I can't see her."

"But you've watched it enough times to know what she's doing, haven't you?" Wanda answered by licking her lips and gently tracing her nipples through the material. "You watch it when you're alone? And then you masturbate?" Wanda blushed, smiled, and arched her back enough to expose the swell of her right breast. Fanny zoomed in and tried to remain the objective director, even as Wanda teased the brown nipple to hardness. "Why do you like this movie so much?"

"It's...she...she gets so...um..." Wanda shivered and seemed to stall. Fanny peeled her eyes away, hard as that was, to glance briefly at the screen, which contained a close-up of the starlet's spread, glistening vulva.

"You like it 'cause she gets nice and wet for you?"

"Oh."

"Does Marc make you wet like that?" Wanda shook her head, and then her lip trembled. "Hey, it's all right." Fanny hesitated, and then reached out to gently brush her hand over Wanda's forehead. "It's okay."

"I really try to please him," Wanda sighed. "I know that he gets frustrated that he can't make me...come."

"A lot of women have that problem."

"Do you? Do you always have orgasms? By yourself?"

When Fanny whispered, "Yes," Wanda scooted up the bed, freeing both breasts from the sheets. Fanny had to squeeze her hand into a fist. "I could help you. Would you like me to help you?"

"Please."

Fanny looked around the room helplessly for inspiration. "I don't know what to do."

"Show me what you do to yourself." Fanny's mouth fell open. She wasn't sure if that was an invitation to show or to tell, and either way she wasn't sure if Wanda was serious or not.

"Turn over on your stomach and spread your legs." Fanny figured that was simple enough, and if Wanda wasn't game then things would stop there. To her surprise, Wanda did as she was told. "Okay. Pull the sheet down."

"Can you do it for me?"

"Yes." Fanny stood at the end of the bed and carefully peeled the thin sheet away, revealing Wanda's full ass. "Move your legs apart." Wanda hesitated, but only for a second. From behind Fanny could see Wanda's nicely trimmed vulva. "Does the air feel good between your legs?" Wanda's hand appeared beneath her as she nodded. "No, don't touch yourself yet." Fanny scanned the room for something soft, and found it on her chest. She removed her satin blouse before she lost her nerve and slipped it into Wanda's palm.

"This is soft. Put it between your legs and—" She didn't want to stop this before it got good, and she had no idea what words she could use that wouldn't turn Wanda off completely. "Gently rub it against your lips."

"My...lips."

"Yes, Wanda," Fanny whispered as she watched her own nipples harden against her bra. "Your labia."

Wanda shivered as she slid the blouse down between her thighs. "Soft." She rubbed the shirt in gentle circles against her pubic bone, then made shy swipes along her outer lips. "Feels good." Her hips pressed forward as she swallowed a shy moan. "Is this your blouse?"

"How do you know?"

"I can smell you on it."

Fanny smiled and knelt between Wanda's spread feet. "Sniff

it." Wanda pulled the blouse to her face and took a deep breath. "Does it still smell like me?"

"Smells like...both of us."

"Put it in your mouth." Wanda's tongue made long, teasing swipes along the material, and Fanny's heart raced as she imagined momentarily that it was her panties instead of her blouse. When Wanda's satin covered hand appeared between her legs again, Fanny leaned down to get a better view. "Press your fingers deeper this time." Wanda spread her lips and rubbed the fabric against her introitus. Fanny's mouth went dry as she watched. "Rub it against your clit."

"Mm." Wanda's hips made tiny pulsing motions against her hand.

"Are you hard?"

"Yes."

"Touch your clit, but don't use your fingers."

Wanda stopped moving. "I don't understand." Before Fanny could offer, Wanda tucked her head in her pillow, tilted her ass up in the air, and whispered, "Show me?"

Fanny started to reply, but she could tell her voice would crack embarrassingly if she did. With slightly shaking hands, she took the blouse from Wanda and held it up by both sleeves. As best she could without touching her, Fanny slid the material loosely over Wanda's genitals. A soft moan escaped her unwillingly as she watched a pearl of fluid trickle down Wanda's pink vulva. "You're pretty."

"You think I'm pretty down there?" Fanny pulled the blouse taut and slid it lengthwise between Wanda's inner labia, long slow swipes from the hood of her clit down to the perineum. Wanda's back arched as she moaned loudly. When Fanny pulled the blouse away there was a large damp spot on it.

"You have a beautiful pussy," Fanny stated as she stared proudly at the fruit of her labor. Wanda sighed and rubbed herself against the bed.

"What does my...pussy...look like?"

"Your outer lips are so full and pink, and the hair looks really soft. The inner lips look like petals. I can't see your clit." Fanny twisted the blouse into a conical shape and moved it gently between the folds, until Wanda groaned louder and left more of her wetness on the shirt.

"Fuck. That feels so good."

"It looks good." Fanny froze for a second, afraid if she let on how hot she'd become that Wanda would freak. "I mean, um, I can tell that you're—"

"Do you want to...touch yourself?" Wanda arched and pressed her crotch against the material in Fanny's hand. She pressed back until the makeshift phallus nudged against her opening. "Fuck. Oh. You can, Fanny. If you want."

Fanny cleared her throat. "This was supposed to be about you."

"I want you to," Wanda whispered.

Fanny was so glad Wanda was blindfolded and couldn't see how hard she was smiling.

"Okay. Don't stop, though. I'm right here watching." Fanny undid her bra and let it slip off her shoulders as she watched Wanda grind back against the balled-up shirt, the folds of cloth running like woven water against her folds of skin. "Shit, Wanda."

"Oh. I wanna...wanna..."

Fanny stood up to remove her shoes and pants. "You wanna what?"

Wanda's moans were louder than her speech, but eventually

Fanny made out, "Wanna...turn you on."

"Ohh." Fanny kneeled on the bed and slid a hand between her legs. She was surprised at how wet she was already. "You are."

"Good." Fanny watched as Wanda spread her lips wide and gently pushed two fingers inside her vagina. "Are you watching my fingers in my pussy?"

"Baby." Fanny sank down on her belly to get a better look. "I see you. I smell you."

Wanda quickly flipped over on her back. She smiled shyly, then scooted closer, until she could feel Fanny's shoulders against her inner thighs. "Is this okay?"

Wanda's pussy opened and glistened less than a foot from Fanny's face. "God, yes."

"Yes." Wanda spread her legs wider and placed her bare hand on her sex. "Do you like how I smell?" Once she'd said it, Wanda blushed and almost giggled. Before she could close her legs, Fanny grabbed them and held them in place.

"Don't. You're beautiful. Don't hide now." Fanny held Wanda's legs until Wanda returned to stroking herself, and then they fell open on their own. She left one hand on Wanda's leg so the other could rub at her own nipples. They shriveled in her hands, wanted to explode once she touched them with saliva-slick fingers. "Fuck yourself again for me." Wanda slipped fabric-covered fingers inside herself, and when she slowly pulled them free the material was dark with even more fluid. "Damn. You're so wet."

"I want to be...I want to be," Wanda groaned as she continued to slide her fingers in and out of her vagina. "Oh... yes...make me wet," she whispered, her head to the ceiling as she leaned on one arm and scooted even closer to Fanny's hungry mouth. "Make me wet." Fanny shoved her hand inside her panties and searched out her erection; it was like glass.

"Lie back," she demanded as she sat up and sucked her fingers. Wanda fell backward and squeezed her breasts as she opened her legs invitingly. "You want me to touch you, don't you?"

Wanda groaned and nodded. "Please. I want to feel you."

"This is what you wanted all along," Fanny declared as she pulled her wet panties aside, growling when the air hit her exposed pussy. "To be with a woman. This was your fantasy all along."

Wanda licked her lips. "Yes. Yes."

"You've never been with a woman before. You thought maybe a woman could make you feel things that your boyfriend can't."

"I thought you could make me feel things that he can't."

Fanny looked down at the sight before her, the open mouth, the open legs, the open pussy, and then she felt a flood in her own hand. "Fuck, Wanda. You aren't wrong."

There were so many places to start, Fanny suddenly couldn't move. She wanted to kiss Wanda, search her mouth, suck on her tongue, taste her pussy on her lips. She wanted to crawl between Wanda's legs and eat her out. She wanted to get the dildo that Wanda surely brought along and fuck Wanda with it until she passed out. She wanted so much at the same time it was dizzying, and all the time her own need was screaming to her from between her legs. It had to be her first; she owed her that much.

Fanny sat back on her heels and pulled Wanda forward. She touched her sex softly, first through the damp blouse and then with her bare hands. Wanda jumped and purred. "That's it. Open up to me. Show me how hot you are." When she slipped her middle finger inside, they both purred. "You're so hot inside."

"Oh. Please."

Fanny pressed her finger in slowly before pulling it out and greedily popping it in her mouth. "Mmm. You're sweet. Your pussy's so sweet." Wanda cried out and blindly grabbed for Fanny's hand, her foot, anything to get the friction back. When Fanny had tasted enough, she touched her wet fingers to the hood of Wanda's clit and gently pushed back, exposing the engorged tip to the air.

"Ah, fuck me. Please, fuck me."

"I will. I want you to get real nice and wet for me first." The blood racing in her own sex was becoming harder to ignore, especially with Wanda's pussy advertising its need all over Wanda's labia, the sheets, and Fanny's mouth. Fanny wanted to get her off so she could get off. She thought about straddling Wanda's face, letting Wanda trace her swollen lips and the protruding tip of her clit through her panties for a while, but she was afraid that might send her over the edge first. And she knew if she crawled on top of her, rode her, crushed their hips together as they ground their pussies together, Wanda might just up and leave her boyfriend.

Fanny shook that dangerous thought from her mind.

"I think I need to make you come right now," Fanny grunted. "I want to watch you masturbate like when you're alone, watching women fucking themselves on your TV, thinking about your boyfriend's cock inside you...or me inside you." Wanda hissed as she rubbed circles around her clit faster and faster. Fanny watched, and then took over, but did it slower, and stroked the swell of her labia rather than the exposed clitoris. "Gentle, Wanda. Like this." She grabbed for the blouse and used it to tease the opening of Wanda's vagina. It thanked her with several drops of fluid.

"Fuck fuck fuck." Fanny smiled and slipped the tip of the material inside Wanda's vagina. When she rubbed the sopping material over the sensitive flesh, more fluid spilled out on Fanny's hand.

"Baby. Look how wet you are."

"I want to see," Wanda groaned as she curved up and lifted the scarf from her eyes. She couldn't see much, but she felt the torrent on her fingers. The more she moved, the more Fanny stroked her with the wet material, the more juices seeped from her sex. She lay back, re-covered her eyes, but she couldn't hide the surprise on her face. "Oh, my god...oh, my god," she groaned as her fingers raced between her legs, "I'm so wet... I'm so fucking wet...I'm so fucking wet!"

"I want to eat you so bad."

Wanda spread her labia apart with her hand and licked her mouth. "Fucking eat me," she grunted forcefully. "Make me come in your mouth."

Fanny took a deep breath and licked her way from inside Wanda's thigh, up to her puffy mons, and then quickly up to her pert breasts. She'd expected the thankful-but-frustrated panting as she suckled Wanda's nipples to hard peaks. What she didn't expect was how hard she was rubbing her crotch against Wanda's thigh. And how hard she was breathing. And she really hadn't foreseen how the sight, the touch, the pungent scent of Wanda's dripping pussy made her own juices rage. She wanted to slow down, take a few deep breaths, but Wanda was rolling and gushing like a river in front of her, and six months was long enough to wait. She pressed her nose and mouth against Wanda's sex, and they both mumbled sharp curses.

"Yes. Fanny, please eat my pussy. Lick me, baby...lick me." As her tongue curled around the swollen inner lips, Wanda fell apart even faster than Fanny could have ever dreamed. "Yes. Right there. Eat me. Eat me. Put your tongue inside me." Fanny held Wanda's thighs in place and gently fucked her with her outstretched tongue. When she looked up, Wanda was alternately squeezing her nipples and sucking on her fingers. Fanny wondered what that would be like, inside Wanda's mouth, but she had to drink her first.

"Watch me eat you." At first Wanda bit her lip like she had to think about it, but when she felt Fanny's tongue flicking against her clit, she howled and ripped the makeshift blindfold off. "Yes," Fanny growled as their eyes met. "Eating your pussy is getting me so damn wet."

"Yeah." Wanda's eyes glistened like her sex. "I want to see for myself."

Fanny replaced her tongue with her fingers, curling them upward to find the urethral sponge. When she pressed into it, Wanda looked like she might cry. "You want to return the favor?" Fanny hissed as she fucked with her fingers and rubbed Wanda's clit with her thumb. Wanda's eyes grew wide. "Tell me what you really want, baby." Fanny opened her mouth wide against Wanda's sex, forming a tight seal so that nothing could stand in the way of her tongue's assault against the very tip of the clitoris. Once Wanda was pulsing against her face and wailing like she was in pain, Fanny growled, "And then you'll get it," and went all out, flicking her tongue and fingers mercilessly at the very base of the clitoris, until she heard it.

"I...I want to fuck you, Fanny." And it was obvious, by the

way Wanda's legs went impossibly wide, by the way her voice went impossibly high, by the impossible amount of hot liquid seeping out of her pussy and all over Fanny's awaiting tongue. She cursed over and over as she came down, hands sliding along the wetness between her legs and underneath her. When she finally stopped moaning, she looked down at Fanny and smiled. "I've never...I got all over the bed."

"You sure did." Fanny looked down at the moisture Wanda left on her chin. Wanda saw it, blushed, then looked down at Fanny's breasts and her damp panties and blushed more.

"Come here," she said, easily. "I want to feel your pussy against mine."

When Fanny climbed on top and felt Wanda rip her panties off, she knew she didn't have long. When she felt the body underneath her, the breasts and the swell of the belly and the stickiness between the legs, she knew she would come before she wanted to, before she'd have the chance to show Wanda how she really liked to be fucked. When Wanda pulled her down and greedily kissed hard and hot and open-mouthed without asking first, Fanny could already feel the warmth spooling below her waist. Then Wanda tilted her hips, and they both arched, and they were suddenly at the perfect angle. She could feel Wanda's sex all sticky and open and warm against hers. She shivered and thrust against her, increasing the friction between her clit and Wanda's clit, her sex and Wanda's sex, her and Wanda. She smiled. "I'm gonna—"

"But I wanted to eat you out first," Wanda murmured, smiling and serious and still so very wet. Fanny saw the promise in Wanda's eyes and in Wanda's hand suddenly buried in her pussy, and she finally fell apart.

An hour later, Wanda peeled herself from the bed. Fanny suddenly felt very naked. "I thought you got the room for the whole night."

"I did, but." Wanda looked at the sheets with a hint of embarrassment. "The sheets are so, um, damp. I can't sleep on them."

"Oh. Yeah, you're right. I guess we can check out early." Fanny clumsily went about finding her clothes, hopelessly trying to ignore Wanda's eyes on her back and the silly lump in her stomach. When she went for the camera, she found it was dead. "Shit. The battery ran out. I don't know how much it got."

"That's okay."

Fanny packed the camcorder in the case. "I'll look at it on my computer and try to burn it to DVD this weekend. When do you want it?"

Wanda walked over and took the camcorder out of the case and turned it over in her hands nervously. "Could I come over and watch it with you? I'd like to see what it looks like. Would that be okay?"

"Sure, but we have to download it to my computer before we can watch it." Fanny held her breath.

"Yeah. I know," Wanda said with a twinkle in her eye, "I have the same camera."

ON LOAN

Lauren Wright

"He'll be in room fourteen-oh-eight," she heard Steve saying over her cell phone. She couldn't tell if he was excited on her behalf, but he had apparently gone to some effort to arrange this meeting.

"Thanks," she answered.

"Have a good time."

"I really think I will," she said with a little smile. "Thanks for everything, Steve. I'm a lucky girl to have you, you know."

"Yes, you are. But you can pay me back later," her lover said, his intonation insinuating there were many delicious ways in which she could thank him for his generosity. "Anyway, you should probably head up. Like I said, have a good time. 'Bye, sexy."

" 'Bye."

She wondered if anybody in the lobby could tell what she was up to. It was hard not to feel self-conscious, hard not to feel like they could look right through her knee-length black trench coat to see the revealing lingerie beneath. She walked to the elevators and entered one that was, she was glad to note, empty. As the floors ticked by, she came to terms with her situation.

She'd always told Steve that she'd love to be lent out. It was a fantasy she'd harbored for years, one that had consumed her on many a lonely night. She pictured herself as a precious toy, one that men would beg for a chance with. Not a hooker, but not entirely independent, either: a coveted, priceless fuck toy to be treated with respect, yet used with abandon. Steve had always promised to make that a reality for her, but when he told her last week that he'd talked it over with a friend who he trusted, she was admittedly surprised. He would be waiting, Steve told her, in the Hyatt. He'd call and give her the room number. All she had to do was show up in something sexy, and let this man take advantage of her. Just the thought of it had sent thrills up and down her belly.

So she'd gone shopping, bought the naughtiest, girliest little piece of lingerie that she could find: a pink push-up bra with little black bows, and a tiny, short matching pink skirt, with garters to hold her black thigh-high stockings up. She'd carefully groomed the satiny chestnut hair that flowed down her back into sexy waves and made up her face artfully. A few sprays of perfume to her chest and back had completed the effect, and made her feel perfect, feminine, and sexy. As the scent of her own perfume wafted up from under her coat, she inhaled and closed her eyes. The feel of the bra pushing her breasts up, the silky lining of her coat slipping against exposed flesh, and the feeling of cool air against her naked cunt was making her heart beat faster already. Walking through the lobby like that had made her feel like a very dirty girl indeed. Now she was heading upstairs to meet a man she'd never met and let him have his way with her. The thought scared and excited her at once.

A little bell rang, and she exited at the fourteenth floor, searching the hall for room 1408. Reaching the door that lay at the end of the hall she stood still for a moment, composing herself. If she didn't knock, she could turn back, but she would regret it forever. She inhaled deeply and knocked, nervously wondering what kind of man waited behind that door.

"Come in," she heard a man's voice speak from inside the room. Apparently, she was to come to him.

Entering the dimly lit room, she tossed her coat aside immediately. Fear and timidity were not what she'd envisioned: this was no place for hesitation. Slowly passing the bathroom to her right, she saw a curtained window straight ahead, and next to the king-sized bed, the shadowy, lithe outline of a man in a well-cut business suit. Her eyes scanned this stranger's well-formed body appreciatively, but stopped abruptly when they met his face.

This man was no stranger. He was someone she'd known her whole life. Often at family parties, always part of her father's gang, he was practically an uncle. Her dad and Nick had been friends for as long as she could remember, and his white smile, tanned skin, and black, now salt-and-pepper hair were ingrained in her mind. How often her little heart had fluttered when she looked at him, how many nights of teenaged angst centered around this eternally handsome man who'd lingered at the edge of her life. She'd come home from school and Nick would be there asking how school was, and she'd stutter and giggle before giving a straight answer. No matter how many boys she'd dated, and how many lovers she'd had, he was always there in the back of her mind. The moment Nick's eyes landed on her they widened in surprise and panic.

"Anna, what are you doing here?" he asked, shock registering loudly in his voice. He averted his gaze and faced the wall.

"I could ask you the same thing, Nick," she answered, just as embarrassed as he was. Raising her hands to cover herself, she began to tap her arm rhythmically. She always did that when she was nervous or worried...some part of her would start to twitch.

"I guess you could at that," he admitted, and looked at her again, his eyes lingering momentarily on her naked skin. He averted his gaze quickly, but it certainly hadn't been a fatherly look. Unbidden excitement trickled its way from her breasts to her thighs in response to that look. Provoked, she lowered her arms to let him see everything: the way her tits pushed perkily out of her bra, the length of her naked torso that ended as the cute, naughty pink skirt began. It barely covered her pussy, and the thigh-high black stockings that ended nearby only highlighted its accessibility. If he was going to look, let him see everything. She wasn't a child anymore.

"Still partial to pink, I see," he commented with a crooked smile. "You have been ever since you were little."

"Don't change the subject, Nick. I'm well aware that you've known me since childhood. We're both in this situation, now what are we going to do about it?" she asked, walking across the room to face him directly. Her skin tingled with his proximity, and the woody smell of his cologne caught her, taking her straight back to adolescent fantasies. As a girl, all she'd imagined was kissing and holding, but those fantasies in the mind of an adult woman now turned to his fingers between her legs, her lips wrapped around him, his cock buried deep inside her. She could feel the wetness and insistent desire building between her thighs. Here he was, a mere two feet from her, and her body was responding so powerfully she could barely control herself. She wanted to touch herself, to present herself to him, to beg for penetration. Still, she held herself in check and watched him coolly.

"Do we need to do something about it? We can both go our separate ways and pretend it never happened, can't we?" he asked, then paused. "I still can't believe it's you that Steve has been talking about these last few months. I had no idea I was hearing stories about Paul's little Anna."

"I'm not little anymore," she responded too quickly, as if she was a teenager again, defending how grown-up she was.

He laughed quietly and stepped closer. She could feel the heat of him and she longed for him to reach out. The image of him naked sprang unbidden into her mind, as she remembered the time when he hadn't locked the bathroom door and she had walked in on him, nine years old and careless. In one shocked moment she'd taken in the length of his muscled, naked body fresh from the shower, before fleeing and telling no one. For weeks afterward, she'd dreamed strange, semierotic dreams that the mind of a nine-year-old couldn't understand. Now here he was, inches from her nearly naked, desperately horny adult woman body and all she wanted was to be bent over and taken. The longing built up painfully, and she had to press her hand into her hip to keep herself from rutting in lust.

"I know you're not little anymore," his eyes traveled her

body again. "That much is clear. What I meant is that I can't imagine Paul's daughter doing the things that Steve told me about. I've heard some rather amazing stories." His eyes met hers again, and she longed to cross the small divide between their two bodies.

She couldn't help being a bit embarrassed by his words. Steve had told him details about their sex life—of course he had—but the thought that her dad's best friend now knew about all of her kinks, all the naughty, perverted things she did in bed, seemed unreal. What did he think of those stories, she wondered. Was he surprised, upset, or excited?

"Did you buy this for tonight, or do you wear it for Steve?" he asked, crossing those final inches and tracing a finger delicately down the strap of her bra. Her body was so sensitive, his touch felt electric. She wished his fingers were elsewhere, slipping on the wetness of her aching pussy. Again she fought the urge to rut.

"It's new."

"Poor Steve, he's really missing something," he spoke thickly. She wondered if he had a hard-on and wished she could touch it, taste it.

"Do you like it?" she asked, wanting to push him further.

"Very much." His finger traced farther down, then suddenly his hand cupped her breast and the other pulled her close, his lips meeting hers firmly, and his tongue seeking out her own. With her body now pushed against his, she could feel the bulging outline of his erection against her hips, and she rubbed herself against it eagerly. Groaning, he grasped her hand and pulled it to his cock, and she began to jerk him off through his pants. He was long and thick, and his whole body tensed with excitement as they kissed and she dry-fucked him.

His hands worked quickly, unfastening his belt and unzipping his pants as they kissed. Pushing his boxers down, he popped his cock out and she sank to her knees immediately to take it in her mouth. His groans, previously quiet, now resounded in the room as she worked her magic, sliding him in and out of her, letting the wetness of her saliva pour down his shaft so that she could stroke him more easily while working his head with her mouth. She sucked his dick like she wanted it all, taking as much as she could, then tugging hard and moving her head in time, rubbing her tongue firmly against the tip of his penis as it pumped in her mouth. She could feel him thrusting gently in time, wanting to push the length of himself all the way in but not wanting to hurt her.

"Put your hands on the back of my head," she ordered, licking his shaft.

"But..."

"No buts, fuck my face," she said, plunging her mouth back over him. Without further argument, his hands went gently to the back of her head and he began slowly thrusting his cock into her, then harder and faster as he realized how much she liked it. She moaned excitedly, still sucking and pumping his cock, never taking in more than she could handle because her hand stopped him from going too far. Slipping one hand to his ass, she felt him thrusting and reveled in his pleasure. He was loving this, fucking her hard and fast, feeling her plump, wet lips around him, and her warm mouth sucking him in. He was so excited she was sure he was going to come, but he pulled back, the length of his rock-hard erection sticking out of his pants in the streetlight that glowed through the window.

Quickly, he shed his clothing, and she saw once again his naked body, muscled and glorious, just as incredible as it had been eighteen years ago. He dropped to his knees too and met her face-to-face as his hand moved purposefully between her open legs to the warm wetness that had only continued to drip as she'd sucked on him. She gasped at his touch, then felt two fingers push firmly inside. She'd needed penetration so badly that just the feeling of his two fingers nearly drove her wild, but as he began to stroke inside her with those two strong fingers, pressing forward against her G-spot, all she could do was moan and fall to her back on the ground.

Not stopping, he leaned forward, and his fingers never left her. Working her hard now, the muscles of his arm pulsed as his fingers probed and stroked her skillfully. She couldn't move, she couldn't think, all she could do was gasp and cry out as each firm pulse of his fingers sent mindless pleasure rippling through her body. She could hear herself squirting, feel the overpowering ecstasy of it as he stroked over and over again, making her back arch and her hands ball uncontrollably into fists. God, she loved it when a man could make her squirt. The pleasure of it sometimes outclassed her usual orgasms, building and building and never letting go, wracking her body in seizurelike waves of tension and release. Clearly Nick had a lot of experience in this arena, and she was loving every minute of it.

His fingers slowed and stopped, and she gazed up at him dreamily, wondering what he would do next. He seemed to be wondering the same thing, so she rose from the ground, and crawled onto the bed, waiting for him to follow.

Just as she'd wanted to before, she presented herself, letting him take in the sight of her wet, blushing pussy from behind, and he responded just as she'd wanted him to. Pulling up behind her, he held the head of his dick against her for one moment of exquisite torture, making her wonder whether he was going to push inside or not. Desperately, she tried to move back and take him in, but he held her ass firmly and backed up a little.

"Please," she cried, pulling her own tits out of her bra so she could tug on her nipples. She wanted him so badly. "Please, Nick, please. I need you inside me."

Giving in, he moved forward, and she sighed with pleasure as every inch of him slid inside. First he gave two slow strokes, and she nearly died from longing to feel it faster. Then his hands wrapped firmly around her hips and he pulled her back as he moved forward, his cock banging deep inside her, the slapping impact of her ass against his hips sending a shocking ripple of pleasure through her body. He started slowly, then built up to a fast, rhythmic pulsing, each time pulling her hips back as he pounded forward, hitting all the right spots inside her fast and hard. Again, she couldn't think, except to cry out words that came unbidden to her lips, "Fuck me, Nick! Be my bad daddy and fuck me hard!"

He growled and pounded her harder with those words, the sheer wrongness of their union driving their lust further. Here he was, a friend to her father who had seen her from childhood, banging her tight little pussy with animalistic abandon. He fucked her with a quick little series of strokes and then reached down to rub her clit with his finger as he pumped vigorously and orgasm overtook her frantically. Pleasure shot from her nipples to her clit, then exploded outward in a rapid, insistent pace that made her whole body shake and rumbled in her head like an earthquake.

Nick kept pumping, and growled again, now with orgasm, as she felt his warm come spill deep inside her. She felt his body hold rigid for a moment as he came, squirting every last drop into her before slipping his cock out and dropping down on the bed in fatigue.

She reveled in the afterglow of their moments together, sexual energy floating in the air, and settling on the pillows beside them. Sitting up, she looked over at Nick inquiringly. "You're not sorry, are you?"

Turning his eyes her way, he considered the question. "No, not at all. It will have to stay our secret, but I'm not sorry."

"Me neither," she smiled, settling back on the bed. They lay together quietly, in the dark, both caught up in their own little worlds. Minutes passed, then an hour, and perhaps one of them napped in the darkness. Then, hungering for more, Anna rolled over and touched his cock. It rose in immediate response to her touch and she leaned forward, taking it again in her mouth and sucking slowly, bringing him back to rigid attention. Moaning softly, he thrust upward into her mouth rhythmically. Pulling his dick against her chest, she looked him in the face.

"Fuck me again, Daddy?" she asked, pouting.

"Mmm, absolutely."

EVE

Alana Noël Voth

She was destined to lead them to Sodom. Him with his God-given prostate. Her with a strap-on cock. Eve's parents had fucked in the open, like animals in the firelight past a girl's bedtime in a house where noise carried, and a girl got out of bed and followed their sounds. She wandered in a nightgown, dragging her fingernails across the acrylic paint she didn't feel come away like skin but like flecks off a ghost, to a living room that opened to a second room with a fireplace.

There, Eve saw bodies oiled in the light, her parents, her mother on top of her father, and her mother was like a banshee with hair like twine. She rode him like that—tethered but pulling loose. Eve knew a phrase from school.

Screw him. She ran to her room and screwed a pillow. She screwed pillows until she screwed men.

In a kitchen, Eve grown up diced an onion on a cutting board and the smell was so strong it burned her eyes. The tears burned her. She could grab her latest lover by the hips, the place he liked so much, right there, thin layer of skin grown thicker since he stopped smoking again, and she could shove him into a wall.

Or, she could be more menacing than that.

Eve's lover had met another woman in Chicago last time he was there: old friend, an ex-lover, something like a bray in a barn or Eve stubbing her toe over and over again.

That annoying infernal anger.

Her lover had been in search of new ways to get control of Eve lately because she was bored, pulling loose; as if her becoming jealous of another woman would do it. He was childish, but he wasn't dumb. The other woman had become like a child who ripped the scab off Eve's sores, exposing holes in her soul, ten thousand years old. Don't tempt me. Eve saw her lover on a gold and red bedspread on a bed in no particular place, and he was an earthen, shaped body; the other woman was a lickety-split vine. Eve smelled leftover whiskey in glasses by the bed and an ashtray crying ashes since he'd started smoking again. Only time smoke left his mouth, when he burned from the inside out.

Ask God about the Garden of Eden. Eve had gone crazy.

She'd grab the bitch by her throat, and her lover's friends would have to try and pull her off the woman he'd met in Chicago.

"It's not my fault!" he'd scream to Heaven.

Eve in the open, no fig leaves now.

Last night, Eve rode a dildo she thought of as Jimmy McNulty from a TV show, "The Wire." He lay beneath Eve Jesus style between her legs looking up in her face and trying not to come because she'd told him, "If you come, I'll kill you." So Jimmy had to decide.

At night her lover brushed Eve's hair. "My mother used to make me do this." He brushed Eve's hair until quills rose on her skin and her hair turned to glazed blood in the moonlight. She took the brush from her lover once then slid the handle along his thigh until he shivered. She struck him with it, which he liked like a priest who whips himself for sinning, like a puppy so tickled it pissed into the ground.

Eve dropped the hairbrush and found a jar by the bed. She anointed her lover's feet, the soles, between the toes, his Achilles' heel even.

He gasped. "Baby."

Eve poured oil in the cup of her palm. She anointed his cock; oiled the shaft, the head, his balls, saw when he closed his eyes like a credulous baby. Children sleeping straight down the hall. Eve oiled his asshole. Crouched between his legs and eased her lover's knees apart: sparse hair around the star. She pursed her mouth then kissed the wrinkled skin of his balls. She moved the balls with her tongue, smelled piss and talcum powder. Until tomorrow, Eve spared him his Baptist Boyhood Guilt.

God preferred him that way. What Eve liked most were his sighs.

Her lover's asshole felt a degree hotter than the rest of him: the difference between Purgatory and Hell. Her finger was like a straw in a hole. Eve pushed far as she could go. Imagine if she'd eaten the man instead of the apple? All this happened to her. Adam rolled on his back. He trembled on the edge of their bed, legs in the air. Eve oiled a silicone cock loaded into a harness that felt like a holster.

In the Garden of Eden the Devil had told her, "A rib maybe, but never his bitch."

HUSH

Jacqueline Applebee

I lost my voice for several months when I was a child. I don't talk about it much. I pledged myself to become an ambassador of silence, and now I use my mouth in other ways.

As a teenager I learned sign language, but even that was too involved. No, I preferred the fluid voice of a human body in motion. I listen to facial expressions, and I read kisses like journals. A long drawn-out groan means more to me than a library of books.

A lack of words however, does not mean a lack of sound. I'll murmur with delight when I eat rose-petal chocolates, I'll sigh when I sink into a hot bath. The noises I make when I come surprise me every time. My mouth holds power, and it is something that I treasure. I choose to be mute only when it pleases me, and it pleases me to communicate without words. Why would I spend my time yapping, when my mouth is capable of so much more?

I long for a silent world and want to draw a hush around me—the quiet is a comfort blanket that muffles the rest of existence into distortion. I just wish I could keep that blanket around me when I dream and am surrounded by the sounds of screaming. I'd cut my tongue out if I knew it would silence my nightmares.

I like my lovers to keep their mouths shut. I have ways to quiet those who cannot help themselves. Take Professor James Fitzgerald, for instance—his Southern Irish accent was mellow and sweet, but he talked far too much. He was the youngest professor in the university and was nothing like his austere colleagues. The professor wore his frizzy black hair in a short ponytail, and he insisted that everyone call him by his first name when they spoke with him. I longed to hear his real voice. I wanted his body to speak to me.

I knew the professor wanted to screw me from the first moment we met. He had come to my accounts office in the basement of the university with an expense sheet. I was impressed; this was something that most other academic staff saw as beneath them, a thing they would get their secretaries to do, but Professor Fitzgerald said that he wanted to get a feel for the place. I think he was secretly checking out the potential for some action. All that blarney wasn't fooling anyone, and I reeled at the volume at which his eyes swept over my round soft curves. However, I heard something else beneath the flirting—the gaps between his lilting words held a hidden concern; he was unsure of me. My silence was a deep pool he could not fathom.

The next day, we sat in the private dining room at the top of the university's oldest building. For almost three hundred years, only the most senior academics had used this space for their meals, but I was allowed in as a guest of the professor's. There were no noisy students here, no clanking pots and pans. I was more grateful than he would ever know.

I savored my carefully prepared meal and enjoyed the sly looks that James gave me. After a short while he started to recommend what I should have for dessert, his voice a low whisper, but it was still too much.

"Hush." It was the first word I had spoken all day. I lay my warm brown hand in James's pale one, and he smiled with surprise when he noticed the card that I had slipped him, with my address and a time written neatly on it.

"Tonight?" he asked softly, and I nodded before rising to leave.

As an ambassador of silence, I always prepare before venturing into new territories. At home later that evening, I set out my supplies before James's arrival, when the real adventure would begin. Ball gags are the main tools of my trade, and I lined them up on the white bedsheets. These were my modest arsenal in the campaign for quiet. I fingered a large hard gag made of resin. It was not really something for beginners, but James was generously proportioned, and it might just fit. I lifted my perforated dribble gag next; that little beauty usually led to a complete loss of composure for whoever wore it. I put my pony-bit gag away; it was more for show than anything else. There would be no theatrics tonight. A few homemade creations were included in the lineup—three knotted scarves were for the more nervous of my lovers. There was one last addition, a rigid dildo made of swirls of blue and white silicone. I adored the firm feel of it inside me, and as a bonus, it had a bulbous base that could double as a gag too.

My thoughts were interrupted by my mobile phone vibrating on the bed. I switched it off and answered the front door.

"Sorry, but your doorbell doesn't seem to be working," James said apologetically. In truth, I had disconnected it when I first moved here years ago.

James stood in my hallway and looked nervously around. He opened his mouth, and I placed a finger to it.

"Hush." I kissed him, pressed the directive inside with my lips and my sweeping tongue. I wanted no words between us. I held his hand and pulled him after me, my footsteps swallowed whole by the thick carpet.

When we reached my small bedroom, James froze on the threshold. He gaped at my collection of sex toys, and then he turned to me smiling a wide naughty smile. I stepped to the bed, and held up the smallest gag in my collection, a soft red sphere that hung from a strip of thin leather. I silently asked him if he wanted this, by raising an eyebrow.

Of all the things that could have happened next, I never expected one of them would be Professor Fitzgerald making a dive to kneel at the side of the bed. He reverently ran his hands over the line of gags. I was shocked beyond belief.

Once I had recovered, I drew the red gag over his face. He arched against the toy and quietly sighed. I read his exhalation like poetry, knew just how he felt. He had found something he loved, and a thing that he never thought anyone else would want to indulge him with. My heart sang at the knowledge that he would be a citizen of my silent world.

James remained on his knees as I buckled the gag, adjusting

it until I achieved the perfect fit. He grunted, and I translated the sound. He adored the full warm sensation, and he loved the liberty of restraint. He was now free to scream until his lungs hurt, and a muffled murmur would be the only thing that anyone would hear. I lifted his hand to my face and kissed the inside of his wrist.

"Welcome," I said with the simple action. "Welcome home."

I shouldered out of my long blue dress and stood naked before the professor. He watched me as I moved but remained on his knees by the bed. I crooked a finger, and he shuffled to me, eyes wide with longing.

James was a tall man, so I could rub my breasts over his frizzy black hair from his position on the floor. He nosed my skin desperately, increasing the speed and the friction with every movement. I could hear my own heart beating as I gyrated against him, a roaring drum in my ears. I grabbed a handful of his wild hair, and he stilled after a moment.

It was now time to open relations with the natives. I sat on the edge of the bed, and James instantly leaned forward, following me. A firm yet gentle hand on his head stopped him, and he looked up at me with a question in his dark brown eyes. I shook my head and opened my legs instead. My fingers reached into my pussy, spreading my lips wide. All my professor could do was to kneel where he was, and inhale my rich scent. This was a special type of communication, animal-like and base, but as I watched his chest expand with an intake of breath, I heard his hunger clearly. I grinned at the soft hiccup as he tried to draw my fragrance deeper. James was a quick study, and I rewarded him by slipping a finger inside myself, only to smear it along his stretched lips, a taste of things to come.

I reached to the collection of toys and produced the pretty dildo. James tilted his head and made an inquiring noise.

"Hush." I placed a finger to his lips and then quickly removed the gag from his mouth. James flexed his lips, working out the stiffness with seesawing motions of his jaw. I gave him a moment before I pressed the dildo to his mouth then pushed the base of it inside. He dutifully accommodated the tool, and when I removed my steadying hand, he bit down to hold it inside him. I almost laughed as James went cross-eyed whilst looking down at the jutting dildo.

I lay fully on the bed and spread my legs once more. My pussy was an open invitation that the good professor accepted, by climbing up to squat at my feet. It took a few tries but eventually he managed to position himself so that he could jam the dildo inside me. The solid feel would have made me speechless, if I wasn't already struck dumb by the moans James emitted with every shove. I could hear other things—my sticky juices made sordid music that I could listen to all day.

My quiet world threatened to shatter with my building climax, and I panted, keened, but I did not scream out. I remembered my place as an ambassador; wherever I go, and whatever I do, a hush should follow. This was my commodity, my skill, and my pure sweet heaven. There were no other words for this, none that I could express in English anyway. I came to the sound of explosions in my head, and James stumbled back, with the dildo protruding from my pussy like the flagpole of my new nation.

"Well, that was different," James said breathlessly. He yanked the dildo out and replaced it with his heated face a moment later. He planted persistent kisses all over my pussy, with urgent open-mouthed phrases. I listened to his dialect as he stroked me with his tongue. Then he spoke directly to me with a kiss to my clit. I willed the involuntary sounds to stay inside me, but every sweep of his tongue brought the start of a scream to my lips. Screams were for my nightmares only; they had no place here. I came once more with my mouth stretched wide, and my hips clenched around the head of a professor.

I fumbled for the dildo and stuck it into my mouth as I came down from my climax. I sucked contentedly and tasted my juices with every slurp.

James wearily climbed up the bed to lie beside me. He kissed my shoulder affectionately, and I gurgled like a baby. But as the sound of childishness touched my ears, a different kind of silence fell over me like a shroud. James seemed to sense my shifted mood, and he pulled the covers over us both. A dozen different gags toppled to the floor and rolled away unheeded.

I listened to James's heart thump against me, like a slow Morse code that I didn't have to decipher. I felt safe and sleepy, and so very satisfied. Maybe that's why I chose that moment to do something that was rare for me. I stepped out of my silent world for just a second, opened my mouth, and I spoke out loud.

"I saw my best friend die when I was eight years old. I screamed at her to move back from the edge of the railway platform, but my words made no difference. She fell in front of a speeding train."

James said nothing, but he wrapped his arms tight around me. I stayed in his embrace until I fell asleep. When my dreams came, they were wonderfully silent.

DECORATIONS

Sommer Marsden

He tells the boy, "The insides of her wrists please."

I barely have to do a thing. I kneel there naked, my black halter dress neatly folded in the corner. I touch him a few times, run my hand up the shaft of his cock, dart my finger over the weeping slit at the tip. When Jake gives me the nod, I take him into my mouth but only for a moment; just long enough for him to feel the heat of my mouth on his cock, my tongue on the helmet.

The boy, for he is only about eighteen, makes a noise low in his throat, a desperate sound. I sink back on my heels and watch his fist pumping the rosy length of his member. When he says, "Now. I'm going to come now," I offer up my wrists. His semen, hot and white, decorates the bracelets of fortune at the crux of my wrists. Warm ropes of pearly fluid decorate the nature-made creases that adorn me there.

Then we are off, Jake and I, to the next club. He buys me a mojito. I cannot wash my hands, nor wipe them clean. I drink my drink with the shiny snail trail of come drying on my skin. He smiles at me and kisses me deeply, his tongue seeking out the tart taste of lime in the depths of my mouth, possibly the taste of another man.

When he sees the next one, his eyes narrow, like those of a predator. He takes my hand, finishes off his beer, and leads the way. "The next one is over there," he whispers. My skin pebbles with gooseflesh; my nipples grow hard under my dress. I sigh. I can't wait for the next one. And what is the next spot, I wonder.

I don't have to wonder long because the next one, who is more man than boy, readily agrees and follows us into the restroom.

I take off my dress, fold it neatly, set it on the back of the toilet tank. I kneel on a toilet seat cover that Jake has put down for me. The harsh white paper protests under my skin.

"The small of her back," he commands, and the stranger, who is a man and not a boy, begins to stroke his uncut cock. I watch as it lengthens and grows. I realize I have never fucked a man who still had his foreskin. I watch and I lick my lips.

"Go on, then," Jake says and pushes the back of my head none too gently. I can imagine his big fist in my dark blonde hair. I can see the black hairs that pepper his knuckles in my mind's eye. I open wide and let the stranger man stick his uncut cock into my mouth.

Only for a moment though, just long enough to get the feel

and the taste, long enough for him to see his dick disappearing into my mouth. To see how long and lean my throat is when he's fucking my ready lips.

His sound is different than the boy's. His sound is high and almost girlish, and he says what he was instructed to: "Now. I'm going to come now..." and I bow down before him as if I am praying to him so he can access the small of my back. I feel the freshets of come shoot over that pale tender skin. Somehow it's so vulnerable there. The small of the back. Which is why Jake chose it in the first place. When he's done, I stay prostrated as if I am waiting for my prayers to be answered. Best to let the decoration he has left start to dry. Preserve the inkblot of come as it is.

Jake hustles him out, kneels next to me, his pants protecting his skin so he doesn't need a paper toilet cover. "It looks like a palm tree," he grunts and then he worms two big fingers into my cunt. I'm dripping wet, and I squirm under him until he uses just the right rhythm and just the right pressure. I cry out my orgasm bent nearly double on the dirty tile floor.

And we're on to the next club.

"Last one," he says and hands me a fresh mojito. This one is too sweet. The bartender used too much simple syrup. I grimace, toss back half, and set it down. Boldly, unlike me, I spot the one I want: tall and lanky, dark blonde hair like mine, striking green eyes.

I nod but say nothing. Maybe the nod will be enough. It is.

Jake leads me over, sips on his beer, whispers in the young man's ear. His green eyes light with greedy glee as he takes me in: my body, my dress, the dried come on my slender wrists. This time it is the coatroom.

My dress is neatly folded; I am kneeling on someone's

cashmere scarf. I like the feel of the sultry fabric under my sore knees. Jake explains, the stranger nods. He feels he must tell us that his name is Todd.

"Right. Todd. Good for you," Jake says. "So when you shoot your load, Todd, you aim for the nape of her neck. Got it?"

Todd bobs his head eagerly and lets his pants fall around his ankles. He strokes his short but wide cock, and it turns purple almost instantly. It's amazing how they are all the same appendage, capable of the same thing, and yet so wildly different.

"Go on, then," Jake says with a laugh and gives my bare asscheek a gentle nudge with the tip of his shoe. "Such a cock slut." The laugh is good-natured.

I give Todd sixty seconds of heaven, sucking his short fat cock. I like the way it fills my cheeks but not my throat, how it's fat but short so I can take it all the way in. I have to wonder if a cock that short would hit the good stuff while he fucked me or if I would be forced to teach him how to get me off with his hand. It doesn't really matter because Todd has been pushed to the brink just watching me suck him.

"Now! I'm going to come now!" he says as instructed. I like that he is the most exuberant of all for the night.

I bow my head like I'm going to kiss his feet and feel his come shoot rivulets along the nape of my neck. I feel it running like warm rainwater in the tendrils of hair that have escaped my hair clip. I sigh at his feet because I can feel Jake's eyes on me. I can feel the phantom touch of his fingers deep in my pussy, and my sex throbs with excitement.

Todd is gone. I am bent and the come is drying.

"A heart with an arrow," Jake says examining it. "I swear to god, it looks like he drew it on purpose. Bullshit though, he damned near had a seizure when he came."

Jake helps me up. I put on my dress. The skin at my nape and my wrists and the small of my back feels tight and constricted from the coatings of dried come.

"Ready?" Jake asks and offers me his arm. I take it and we go.

The Blacklight is his favorite club. And for a reason. Inside the black lights make all kinds of things glow. They make me glow, not for the first time. I turn my wrists up like a prisoner and see the glowing white stain of come. He spins me to the mirrored wall and holds my compact up. I see the heart with the arrow glowing at the nape of my neck, bits of my hair, shiny and surreal, glowing white like a beacon. He lifts my dress because in this club no one really gives a shit. Above my black thong is the palm tree, like a cosmic tattoo, glowing in the lights like a million tiny stars glued to my skin.

Jake walks me into the corner. The black light penetrates but very few nosy gazes can. He hikes up my dress and slides my thong to the side. His big fingers find me wet and ready. He takes his wet finger and works my clit until I am bucking against the mirrored wall, my reflection shining back at me, crazy and cut up. Over the thumping music I hear his zipper, feel the big blunt head of his perfect cock work at my hole. I arch my hips, hook my ankle behind his back and pull, eager for him, a slut for him.

"Easy, Lisa," he laughs. He's laughing because he knows I can't be.

He goes slow, lets his eyes sweep over the decoration at my wrists, lets his fingers sweep over the one on my back like he's reading Braille. I know he can see my nape in the mirror.

"You look so fucking hot when you're all decorated," he

says and slams into me. For just a second my feet leave the floor with his force and I don't care. I wrap my legs around his waist as he fucks me hard, ramming my back into the reflective wall as I cling to him.

"Now. I'm going to come now," he says with an evil laugh, mocking my suitors for the night.

He comes with a growl and I come with him, around him. The dance beat that is thumping in my ears and my head swallows up my cries as I come not once but twice, Jake shoved deep inside of me, the taste of three strange cocks and two bad mojitos still on my lips.

THE GIRL NEXT DOOR

Kay Jaybee

"Get down on your knees. I want to see you crawling."

He looked at her; surely she was joking. Her green eyes had narrowed to hard flint slits. No, she wasn't joking. He dropped onto all fours, his bare legs cold against the tiled bathroom floor.

Jack should have asked her what the hell she was doing in his house. He should have demanded to know why she was barging in on him in the bathroom when he was about to shower, but the words caught in his throat at the sight of her. It was as if a stranger stood before him, not Kim, the girl he'd known for so long, the quiet girl that lived next door.

On his hands and knees he hovered below her, self-conscious that his dick was stirring, swelling under her piercing gaze. Despite the two pints of beer he'd had that evening, his mouth had gone dry, and he licked his lips apprehensively as he waited to see what would happen next.

Kim, her hands on her hips, observed the object of her fantasy as he crouched beneath her. She had to struggle not to smile as his naked body responded to her presence. She'd dreamt of this, frequently imagining what Jack would look like underneath his habitual jeans and T-shirt. She wasn't disappointed.

For years Kim had waited with a quiet desperation for Jack to notice her, always there, always a friend in a crisis. He had never truly seen her though, never noticed her against the background of silicone enhanced blondes he brought home at distressingly frequent intervals. She'd had enough. If she was going to move on, she had to have him, just once. Just to see if the reality could be as good as the dream. So, pushing past the boundaries of right and wrong, Kim had allowed her obsession to guide her. Using the key that Jack had given her for emergencies, she had let herself into his home and waited for his return from the pub, praying that he'd be alone. Her dubious request answered, Kim, clad only in a maroon basque and stockings and suspenders, with her long black hair in two tight pigtails, hid and waited.

Kim's pulse drummed against her chest, and her voice sounded husky and strange as she spat out her next order. "Kneel up."

Jack obeyed, his cock swaying toward her like a compass needle, his whole body rigid with expectation and uncertainty. His deep blue eyes bored into hers, questioning, but he didn't quite dare to speak, as if he knew that any sound from him would break the spell and end this—whatever this was.

Kim, her hands still on her slim hips, widened her legs slightly and said, "Lick me."

Her words cracked against the tense silence as Jack, hesitating for only a fraction of a second, crawled toward this new Kim, one who was unexpectedly, deliciously in control, and expecting obedience. Feeling her slick clit harden beneath his tongue, Jack's mind raced. He'd had no idea she liked him in this way. On the other hand, until this evening, he'd had no idea he wanted her either.

Kim closed her eyes tightly as Jack lapped at her. Steadying himself by grasping her legs, trapping the clips of her suspenders beneath his palms, he swirled his tongue over and around her pussy, making her sway against the exquisite pleasure. Allowing herself to relax against his attention, Kim came quickly, her mound pressing against his wet face as she shuddered to a swift climax.

Taking a deep breath, Kim took a step back and forced herself to look hard at Jack. An expression of mild shock had settled on his face. *Good,* she thought, *I've surprised him but not, happily, repulsed him.*

Speaking quickly, whilst her body recovered from its welcome attention, Kim pointed to the bath. "Bend over it."

This time Jack hesitated longer, unsure how he was supposed to carry out her instruction, but as it seemed unlikely that further information was going to be forthcoming, he shuffled on his knees across the hard floor, and leaned over the white plastic panel.

"More." Kim pushed his firm backside higher into the air, forcing his stomach farther across the bath, so that his hips were uncomfortably level with the top of the panel, his weight supported by his arms on the bath's far side.

"You will not move." Kim ran a newly painted red fingernail down his buttcrack, and felt a thrill of power as Jack shivered beneath her touch. "Nor will you speak."

Ignoring his nod of agreement, Kim picked up the hairbrush she knew Jack always kept in his windowsill, and familiarized herself with its pleasing weight. This was the part of her plan she'd dreamt of most, the punishment he was so long overdue. Punishment for not having seen what was right under his nose.

Kim struck the first blow and watched in fascination as Jack's skin puckered beneath the blow. The second hit made his right buttcheek glow. Kim stopped again to see how the flesh blotched with pink. By strike four she had got into her stride, and Jack's stoic whimpers had became grunts and groans of bitten-back agony.

Another blow, and another. One for each of the girls he'd brought home in the weeks since Kim had first hatched her plan. One for each girl he'd shagged that wasn't her.

It was the tenth blow that broke him. Tears gathered unbidden at the corners of his eyes, and Jack raised his blond head. Heedless of her request for no words, he cried out, "Stop. Kim, please! What are...?"

Cutting across his pleas, Kim spat out in a fierce whisper, "I told you not to speak."

"I..." Jack spluttered, desperately aware that, despite the burning across his backside, his submission had turned him on far more than he'd expected it to, as Kim's tightly calm voice interrupted him again.

"You haven't been punished enough yet."

"But I..."

"You spoke again! Oh, dear." She feigned mock resignation. "I feared this might happen. Stand!" Her ordered cracked out, echoing around the pristine white-tiled walls.

Jack, bruised and dizzy from the blood that had rushed to his head, rose steadily to his feet. His brain seethed in a ball of confusion: why was he being punished? What had he ever done to upset Kim? He wasn't sure of anything, least of all why he didn't protest, why he didn't just step forward in his usual confident manner, rip the basque from her chest, and attack the breasts that were visibly swelling beneath. His heart pounded in his ears with the need to penetrate this surprising creature, but curiosity and bemusement kept him exactly where he was.

Kim walked around Jack, appraising his body with a critical gaze, making him feel like a beast being examined for market. Then, standing directly in front of him, she unclipped her stockings and, infuriatingly slowly, rolled them down and off.

His eyes followed her fingers as Kim deftly folded the nylon in half and approached Jack. Understanding her intention, he took an involuntary step backward. Kim looked at him coquettishly through her long black eyelashes. "You aren't afraid of me, are you?"

The challenge in Kim's words made Jack stand still, and after a second's indecision, he cautiously allowed himself to submit to her. Silently he parted his mouth so she could gag him with the soft material.

Not waiting to admire her handiwork, Kim took the second stocking and, after stretching it out slightly, used it to bind Jack's wrists behind his back. Then, leaving him behind, she walked out of the bathroom and into the bedroom, and waited for him to follow her.

Kim had never been in this room before. Standing by Jack's double bed, she quickly assessed the space available to her as she waited for his arrival. He appeared then, standing sheepishly in the doorway of his own room.

"Get back on your knees," Kim hissed, "no one gave you permission to stand."

Jack stumbled clumsily to the floor, confused at his enjoyment of the situation. As he reached the bed, having successfully managed not to burn his knees on the rough brown carpet, he rocked back onto his haunches, feeling rather like a faithful dog waiting for its mistress to give it permission to play.

As if reading his thoughts, Kim patted him on the head, feeling the spikes of his gelled hair against her palm. She spoke softly this time. "You're a very naughty boy. Do you know why you're being punished?"

He shook his head quickly, his eyes wide with an odd combination of expectation and unease.

Kim trailed a finger across his cheeks. "I didn't think you did." She walked over to his desk and picked up a long plastic ruler, flexing it slightly between her hands. A surge of pleasure shot down her spine as she witnessed a flicker of fear cross Jack's face. "You see, I've been waiting for so long. That was your big mistake. Not really seeing me."

Jack gulped against the gag. This felt like stalker territory. He should stand and run, but he felt hypnotized by the ruler Kim was flexing between her fingers.

"I've watched you bring them home, all your bottle blondes." As she spoke, Kim's eyes burned with the most all-consuming lust Jack had ever seen. "A long procession of disposable wasted sex. All that time I was next door, waiting for my turn;

waiting with all the fucking you could ever need."

Kim reached out a hand and gripped his cock, making Jack groan through the stocking as she squeezed him hard. Treating his dick like a dog lead, she pulled at it so Jack was forced to stumble to his feet. Kim ran her fingers up and down his length with one hand, and smacked the ruler against his already sore buttocks with the other. "Two more strokes for the last two tarts you serviced."

Jack bit into the gag, the twin sensations shooting sparks of longing through his body. Then suddenly she stopped, pushed him back to his knees, and gently, as if now that his punishment was over all her anger had evaporated, engulfed his dick between her parted lips.

Alternating between light licks and grating nips, sucking lips and deep-throated pumps, Kim heard Jack whimper into his gag as the first flecks of precome salted her tongue. She pulled away, noticing the growing blush of red against his pale smooth chest. He was so close now.

Standing back up, Kim saw a look of frustrated disappointment cross his face. "You'd like me to do that again wouldn't you?"

He nodded vehemently, all pride gone in the face of his need to feel her mouth against him.

She smiled at him wickedly, twirling her pigtails between her fingers, "Perhaps if you're a good boy, I'll do it again sometime."

Her hands came to her basque, and Kim began to untie the laces that held her chest captive. Without saying a word, but keeping her eyes locked on to Jack's, Kim freed her tits, rolling her nipples between her fingers. They grew beneath her touch as she changed from gentle fondling to hard kneading, making her pussy tingle and juice leak down her legs.

"Would you like to touch these?"

Again Jack nodded urgently, as she held her breasts up before his face.

Kim moved her hands down to her thighs and, sitting on the edge of the bed, deftly removed her knickers. Spreading her legs wide so he could clearly see her wet sex, Kim leaned back, displaying herself more effectively as with one hand she continued to massage her nipples and with the other, finger her clit, writhing herself to an orgasm.

Jack sat, transfixed by her performance, cowering pathetically and waiting for permission to move, silently wishing for some desperately needed attention of his own. He was so aroused by Kim's display that he was worried he would come there and then, and never feel that luscious body next to his.

As the sighs of her second climax ebbed away, Kim rose to stare at her captive. "My word, aren't you horny. Look at that dick; you'd like to put that in here wouldn't you?"

Her crudeness as she pointed to her still-flushed sex made Jack even hotter as he nodded again; the nylon in his mouth was becoming increasingly sticky as he helplessly dribbled into it.

She laughed at him. "Well, my slave, I could be cruel. I could punish you longer for all those years of bodily neglect," Kim flashed a cold glare at his pleading eyes, "but that would only be punishing me as well, and right now I badly want to feel that cock inside me."

She signaled for him to lie down on the floor. Jack shook his bound arms in protest, but she dismissed the problem, "It'll be a bit uncomfortable for you, but you'll manage I'm sure."

Jack clumsily lowered himself onto his back. Rapidly Kim

sat astride him, impaling herself on the cock she'd fantasized about for so long. Doing his best to ignore his squashed hands and aching arms, Jack lifted his hips to try and jam up against her, but Kim slapped them hard. "I did not say you could move."

Relishing the feel of his body trapped within and beneath her, Kim slipped a hand down to fondle his balls where they touched her body, smoothing and caressing Jack and herself at the point of conjunction. Jack gave a muffled moan as he watched her sitting victorious above him.

Then, as if every atom of self-control within her had snapped, Kim began to hammer herself against Jack's prone body, screeching in ecstasy as he fired his spunk into her quivering body.

Lying flat on top of him, Kim yanked away the gag and fell on his mouth with a ferocious frenzy of kissing, nipping, and biting, which he hastily returned in kind. Struggling out of his stocking ties, Jack brought his arms around Kim, scratching and pinching her body and tugging at her pigtails as they rolled around his bedroom floor in a vicious orgy of activity.

As they attacked each other with an angry hunger of want and lust, Jack was consumed with the overwhelming urgency to make up for all that wasted time. Kim had been right; all those hours of passing sex now seemed so pointless—when he could have been right here being bruised, scratched, and deliciously humiliated by the quiet girl next door.

RITUAL SPACE

Janine Ashbless

"You think I'll fit in there?" Hayden asked. He was grinning, but his eyes betrayed doubt. "Seriously, Alex. It's not going to be a problem, is it?"

I glanced at the hole near our feet, a narrow slot about two feet wide and rather less high between the stone floor and the wall of the pit, and then I looked Hayden over, head to toe, just because for once I had a legitimate excuse to do so. "Are you claustrophobic?" I asked.

My team leader topped six feet, though he could otherwise pass for a local—at least until he spoke. Then he became American, and the vendors of tourist junk who'd ignored him before would come crowding round him too, just like they'd been doing round the rest of us. He was half Turkish and half Pennsylvania

Dutch according to site gossip, and one-hundred-percent dark-eyed, disheveled, self-deprecating charm. I didn't suppose I was the first female student on the dig to have a thing for him. Now we were alone together—and my body was horribly conscious of this fact. Everyone else was off hiding from the blaze of the Anatolian sun before the afternoon shift, but we had shade down here in the pit.

"Claustrophobic? Not normally." He indicated our surroundings. We were twenty feet below ground-level, and the pit-chamber was bell shaped so that the walls hung in over us. A shaky aluminum ladder was our only connection to the world overhead, the sunlight and the parched earth and the ruined walls of the excavated town. If he'd been claustrophobic he'd have been panicking already.

"You'll be fine," I told him. "You're not going to get stuck. Just go in feet first. There's a short slope down to the chamber: it's wider down there but not high enough to sit up in. And I can get on hands and knees but I'm not sure you'll be able to." I risked another gratuitously appraising glance, wishing I could tear off his ancient Nirvana T-shirt and his khakis. "To come back out you'll have to roll over onto your stomach and crawl on your elbows."

He blew out a breath. "Sounds...great. Hard hats?"

"They fall off the moment you lie flat. Just keep your head down."

"Okay."

"It'll be worth it. I promise. You have to see this." I was the only person who'd been down into that chamber, though there'd been several of us clearing out the ancient debris that choked the main pit. As the smallest, slenderest person on the site I'd volunteered to work in the cramped conditions of the lowest level and everyone else had been happy to let me do it—besides, there were mosaics to uncover only a few hundred yards away, and all the diggers wanted to be in on those. Mosaics were sexy; they looked good in newspaper articles and on the covers of important journals. Archaeologists get very excited over them. At first this hole in the floor of the Byzantine-era warehouse had been assumed to be a midden and of no importance except for the rubbish thrown into it. When it was found to be too deep and cut from solid bedrock the professors postulated a well-shaft or a grain-store. But my excavation of the subchamber was going to change all that. I was trembling inside.

"I hope you're right," said Hayden.

"I'll go first and switch the lights on." I sat on the rock floor, scooting my butt until my legs were swallowed by the hole. Hayden's head above me was framed by a halo of perfectly blue sky. I had to clear my throat before I spoke again. "You're going to love it," I promised. Then I wriggled into the tunnel and slid down into darkness just as I had done so often before.

The chamber at the bottom met me with its chilly clasp. I rolled to my right and groped for the battery pack, switching on the lamp. Then I shuffled backward out of the way of the entrance.

"Lights on! Come on!"

Hayden came down with a great deal of scraping, his boots emerging first. Lying flat he filled the chamber end-to-end. The first thing he did was put his hands up against the roof, and the second was to try and bring his knees up; when the latter proved impossible he took deep breaths and ran his hands over his face. It was so quiet and we were scrunched in so close that I could hear the rasp as he rubbed his stubble.

"Okay?" I asked softly. I was used to the cramped conditions, but for the first time in my life I'd seen long legs and broad shoulders made a vulnerability, not an asset. He turned his face to mine and grinned, not entirely happily. We were as close as lovers lying in bed.

"Fine. How long did it take you to clear this?"

"About a week."

"Christ!" He laughed. "You deserve a medal." He bit his lip, eyes sparkling. "Well, I can guarantee Professor Czajkowski won't be coming down here to check on your technique."

Since the professor had such an ample girth that he had problems kneeling to dig, that thought was too much for me and I giggled, covering my mouth. "Don't!"

"It's...sorta cosy, Alex. Will it take long to show me round?"

"Hold on." The lamp was on Hayden's far side, and the bulk of his torso was casting deep shadows. I reached over him to grab the battery pack and bulb. My breasts squashed against his chest. "Sorry," I muttered.

"Hey, don't apologize."

We grinned at each other, self-consciously. I was feeling giddy. I deposited the lamp between us. "Okay," I said, my voice a little unsteady: "take a look. Artificial excavation—see the squared-off corners?"

"Uh-uh. A grave, d'you think?"

"No—or at least there's no sign of human remains."

"You're sure of that?"

"It was just full of the same debris that choked the main pit. None of it older than late fourth century. Now take a look at this." I moved the lamp to the side, throwing the texture of the rock ceiling into relief.

"Oh...yes!" hissed Hayden appreciatively. Carved over his head in high relief was a phallus, complete with bulging testes and a clearly defined glans. "Ladies and gentlemen, we have a ritual object."

"You'll see that it's polished smooth compared to the surrounding rock," I said, reaching to run my hand gently along its considerable length.

Hayden made a noise in the back of his throat and I blushed, withdrawing my hand. Fingertip sweat can cause damage even to stone objects.

"Um. I think it's been handled a lot by whoever came down here."

"Fertility ritual," he said hoarsely. "The virile member buried deep in the earth to make it fertile." He scratched his throat, musing. "Or perhaps it's nothing that obvious. In the pre-Christian Empire the phallus was a good-luck symbol of protection from evil—a *fascinum.*"

"I have a theory." I was shy but determined. He turned his head to look me in the eye. We were both sweating a little and breathing quickly in the stuffy air. Only the chill of the stone kept this constricted and intimate space from growing too warm. "I think this is an oracle," I said.

"Yes?" He actually sounded interested. It's not often a student theory gets that far.

"Do you remember the description of the Oracle of Trophonius? It's described as a pit with a narrow hole at the bottom into a deeper passage. Supplicants were pulled in feetfirst and granted information about the future though a vision or a voice. And they came out babbling and terrified."

"Pausanias," he said, nodding. "But that's from the *Description of Greece.* This is Turkey."

"Think about it: this place is identical to his description. And from the right era, though it was obviously abandoned and backfilled after the changeover to Christianity. I'm thinking it could be a cult with more than one site."

"Maybe." His eyes were all dark glitter. "And the visions?"

"This is ritual space: anything could happen here. The supplicants would be lying alone in the pitch dark. Keyed up. Hyperventilating because they're scared and claustrophobic and horny and there's not much air. Reaching out to touch the protective sigil above them. They'd be capable of seeing things even without priests prompting them."

Hayden rolled carefully onto his side to face me, his shoulder nearly brushing the roof. "Horny?"

I shrugged, thinking that my words had run away with me. "Perceived peril makes people more aroused. It's freshman psychology."

He raised his eyebrows. "Well, thank god it's not just me then."

I laughed, mostly from tension, and he chuckled with me.

"So...Did it make you horny, working down here?" he wondered.

I blushed and ran my tongue across my lips. "Sometimes." My voice sounded weak. "It's the silence..."

"Did you ever do anything about it?"

Those eyes would not let me go. I bit my lip and nodded.

"Down here?"

"Yes," I whispered.

He grinned, soft and slow. "I'm not sure that's good archaeological practice."

"No," I admitted. Our voices were very low now.

His face moved closer to mine. "I want to know what you

did, Alex...when you should have been working."

"Why?"

"Professional curiosity." But the sweep of his lips was a caress described on the air. My skin tingled.

"I...would sometimes touch myself."

"Through your panties?"

"Sometimes. Or I would pull down my fly and...touch myself properly."

"Ah. Were you wet before you started?"

"Usually."

"Are you wet now?"

I nodded.

"Show me." His eyes were shining. "Show me how you did it."

For moment I just held my breath. Then, hardly daring to think, I lay back and pulled up my T-shirt, revealing a flat stomach glazed with sweat and speckled with grit. Hayden watched entranced as I thumbed open my fly button and tugged at my zip.

"Left-handed?"

"Uh-huh." Pushing down my trousers and panties to my hips, I shimmied out of them far enough to reveal the tufts of hair at the crease of my sex. Softly I touched myself. Hayden ran the tip of his tongue between his teeth. I could hear his breath coming fast and shallow. I could smell my own musk.

"Yes," he sighed, then reached to draw my top up higher, taking my Lycra bra with it as he found the thicker fabric, pushing both layers right up to reveal my breasts. They felt cold beneath his warm hand. His fingers moved on my sweat-slicked skin, then withdrew. My nipples tightened, aching for the touch they'd known so briefly. "Go on."

I pushed my fingertip into my own wetness, drawing the moisture up to my clit. I was wet with a fierce, boiling heat. I began to play with myself, watching him watching me, seeing how his eyes swept from my quivering tits to my tilted pussy and back to my face. Feasting on his hunger, on the rapt concentration I'd only ever seen him direct at newly discovered artifacts before this moment. Under his gaze I felt as if every inch of my skin was alive with significance. My fingertip rolled over my burning clit, back and forth. I didn't want it to end, but I knew it wouldn't take me long; I'd been building up a sexual charge since he joined me in the pit. I felt my orgasm heave deep within me, reaching toward the surface, and then he obliged by covering my working hand with his, cupping my fingers and my pubic mound and my wetness for a moment before sliding two fingers deep into me. Already on the edge, I came at once with that first electric clitoral climax; he felt my muscles clench on him, pulsing, as I arched my back and cried out.

The stone roof echoed my voice, distorting it strangely.

But he wouldn't let me down afterward. Even as I slumped he pushed my finger out of the way with his thumb and went to work on my folds, my clit, and my open sex, the muscles of his arm bunching all the way to the shoulder. His hand was calloused from digging, but deft. And very strong.

"I want to touch the *fascinum,*" I moaned as his fingers scissored inside me.

"Go on then."

With effort I rolled to face him and pressed my hand to his worn trouser fabric and the cock that strained beneath that. He was hard and heavy and thick with wanting that touch. He groaned and laughed.

"Think this'll be good luck?" I gasped, wrestling open his clothes. He kissed me and I tasted the harsh Turkish coffee he'd had after lunch.

"Oh, yes—that feels like good luck."

"You think..." I finally managed to open his waistband and pull him out into the open. He felt as hard as the stone phallus in my hands. "Oh, god, yes." His cock stood proud, with skin of hot velvet, as meaty as you could ask for. I explored the entire length, smoothing the ooze of moisture from the tip, then pumped him, loving his noises of tortured pleasure, loving the veined hardness beneath my hands and the fat tight pouch of his scrotum. He was full to bursting. But he never let go of my sex, never lost sight of his goal there. His hand twisted inside me and worked in and out on a slippery tide of my cream. The lamp, crushed between us, sent crazy shadows leaping as we moved. I could feel the play of the muscles in his forearm as I tossed his cock, our wrists interlinked in an arm-wrestling match in which we both sought the final throw together.

In the end I fell first, unable to resist his relentless assault, coming in helpless spasms on his hand. He inhaled my cries and came himself, his ejaculate shockingly copious, escaping through my fingers to jet in hot splashes on my belly. It mixed with the ancient dust of the oracle. Behind my eyelids dark spaces flashed and unfurled, landscapes reeled and tumbled.

Afterward, both of us breathless and drenched in sweat, he rolled me onto my back and massaged his semen into my skin, his hand heavy.

"Okay. I'll verify your find, Alex."

"One hell of a find," I mumbled, stroking his cock. It didn't seem too eager to sink back to sleep.

He laughed. "I can't see that the professors would appreciate you taking them that one. How about we wait a bit?"

"I'm not going to them like this," I protested mildly. "I need a shower. Now."

He touched my nipple, circling it with the tip of his finger. "I'll join you."

My solar plexus did a little flip-flop. "Not much room in those shower cubicles," I said lightly.

"So?" His smile was full of promise. "We managed fine here. Imagine what we can do where there's room to stand up."

FAST CAR, NOT FOR SALE

Trixie Fontaine

I don't know why the boys thought my car was for sale, parked roadside in deep grass, undriven so long that yellow jackets had taken up residence in nests behind the side mirrors. Neglected, yes, but for sale? No.

Living three blocks from the high school, we got more than our fair share of small-town traffic, usually boys skirting the lone patrolman by taking our side road. Ogled by older friends picking up younger friends, kids skipping school, unemployed young men haunting their alma mater—my royal buttrock blue, turbo-charged sex-wedge sat hot and lonely in the sun, tempting these drive-by boys to try to claim her.

Working from home as a webmaster, I didn't miss driving her, not much anyway. My boyfriend and I had a practical four-door to do errands around town in and the old Ford pickup for his work. It seemed wasteful to pay for insurance on the frivolity of a third car with no air bags simply for the thrill of being able to go from zero to sixty in six-point-nine seconds. My job kept me contentedly hidden at home, moving slowly in slippers from one room to the next, talking to no one but the dog while Lee was away at work. I didn't really think about my car; it became part of the outdoor landscape I never lifted my computer room's blackout curtains to see. I was only forty years old, and yet I spent my days shuffling around silently like my grandma in her housecoat. My mom called my shut-in lifestyle a shame, but I called it cozy.

Once I found an unzipped backpack discarded in our huckleberry bushes. I guessed it had been stolen from one high schooler by another, ransacked, and the bag with its undesirable paperwork remains thrown out of a car driving past. I was going to take it to the police in case the owner was looking for it but for some reason I never did. I just kept it for a while until the sight of it embarrassed me, making me feel like an accessory to a carelessly executed petty crime.

Another time I heard voices in our yard, but they weren't traveling past the way they usually did when the kids walked by after school. I cracked the curtains an eyeball's width apart and saw three carless teenaged boys investigating my derelict vehicle, one of them sticking a slab of cardboard under the windshield wiper. I waited until they were gone to retrieve the message: *How much for your car?* accompanied by a phone number.

I then considered my car from a new perspective, as something desirable. For the past year she'd just been something I worried our wealthier neighbors would view as an eyesore. My car from the eighties was like a declaration of our low class and status on the block: just renting, with a collection of beater cars the only thing we owned. She gave everyone who looked at her a tasteless wink, one headlight shut tight and the other busted pop-up permanently open. My car was no prize, but I felt sentimentally attached to her. I'd been proud of paying cash even though it hadn't been much, since I got her used.

Since I owned her completely and had no intention of selling her, I'd decorated her bumper early on with a few stickers: a Southern Culture on the Skids band promo, a topless cartoon woman astride a CRT monitor with keyboard in the foreground, and the words WHITE TRASH proudly emblazoned against a field of holographic silver. MY car. It irritated me the way these boys assumed she was up for grabs, the way they thought they could possess her when I'd never even indicated she was for sale. I told myself it was typical male thinking, to look at everything that caught their eyes as something they could own.

I didn't call the boy's number. Anyway, it would be irresponsible to sell such a fast car to such young men, hell-bent on driving with inexperienced recklessness. It was safer for everyone if she just sat there with two wheels sinking into the yard.

The warm weather and the boys looking longingly at my car motivated me to get it fixed up and in driving condition again so I could enjoy her as much as they wanted to. We got rid of the bees, rolled her out of the weeds, and gave her a jump. We didn't give her a proper drive because she was still uninsured, but I liked knowing I *could* if I really wanted to. I remembered how often I used to get honked at and hit on when I was driving her. One time a girl who looked just like a young Sissy Spacek leaned her small-breasted torso out of the passenger window of a car that was pacing me and made the crotch-licking hand gesture at me, her tongue lashing the *V* between two of her fingers before she stopped to scream, "You're beautiful!" Her strawberry blonde hair whipped her face when the driver zoomed ahead and away from me. It had been a long time since a stranger gave me such an obscenely generous compliment.

I decided to work harder than before to make enough money to justify insuring the car. I spent hours inside at my machine, designing and building websites, blogging, and daydreaming about making a new cherry air-freshener spin in my car while I zipped around corners, windows down. I would work for ten hours without talking to anyone or going outside except to check the mail or maybe pick some berries for my oatmeal in the morning. No one came over, and on good days no one called so I didn't have to bother swearing at the phone while I waited for it to stop ringing before going on with work.

Nobody ever knocked on our door either, unless it was the mailman delivering a package, so when I heard four business-like knocks I expected to open up and see a box on the stoop and the rear of my mailman as he climbed back into his van.

It's astonishing how much space two teenaged boys can take up in a doorway. It was like a wall of boy in front of me, blocking out the sun. Suddenly I became aware of my heavy boobs hanging braless under my white T-shirt.

"Hi there, ma'am—is that your car out there? The blue one?" The older boy did the asking. His white T-shirt was identical to mine and he looked completely covered so I don't know why I felt so exposed wearing the exact same thing. Oh yeah, my big old knockers stretched out the front of my shirt making it noticeably different from his stretched out at the shoulders.

"Yes, that's my car," I anticipated him, "...but it's not for sale."

"Is something wrong with it? Because I'm good with cars and maybe I could fix it." I couldn't tell if he was offering to repair it so I could drive it myself or to convince me that he would buy it even if it weren't running. His friend looked away from us both.

"Nothing's really wrong with it I don't think...I mean, it probably needs some work at this point, but it's not for sale."

"Oh."

He just stood there, fingertips in his pockets and knuckles curved out, looking down at an overgrown shrub by the steps. His dark eyebrows slanted down over eyes squinted into slits of concentration, his lips pursed into a determined *V* while he apparently tried to think of another angle. He had a couple days' worth of stubble along his jaw and arching over his mouth, and the humble muscles of a kid who played baseball at one point but now might just buss tables or mow lawns. Young, fresh, yard-work muscles; the kind you don't see in gyms.

When he did look at me again, he looked at my eyes. "Well, my name's Jesse, and I work down at the Olympic Inn Eatery if you change your mind. I could really use something to get back and forth to work."

A week later I found a note written on a guest check ripped off of an order pad tucked into our screen door:

Hey this is Jesse the guy interested in your car. I have no car and I need one so if you don't want to sell call me and let me know so that I can find something else! Thanks —Jesse (368-5830)

What a persistent little fucker! Didn't I already say it wasn't for sale? But I was happy; the thought of calling him excited me. In fact, I'd been excited all week long just imagining the different pornographic scenarios that could have played out if I'd invited him and his friend inside instead of dismissing them as I had. Why don't you boys come on in and see if we can nail down an agreement! Of course I'd allowed myself to imagine these things only because I thought the opportunity had safely passed.

Looking at Jesse's phone number sitting right next to where he'd signed his name in awkward cursive brought a new introduction to my fantasies into reality. I, a grown woman, could call this fresh-out-of-high-school boy.

What if he still lived with his parents and one of them answered? *Is Jesse home?* What if they could tell I was grown-up; wouldn't they wonder why I was calling him? I'm calling because he wanted to buy my car. Of course. I would be calling about the car, not because I wanted to fuck their son. Not because my boyfriend and I had an open relationship that I'd never taken advantage of. Not because I'd gotten off with my eyes shut, one hand between my legs strumming my clit furiously and the other groping my own boobs through my T-shirt, imagining his boy-paws all over me, ripping my shirt up over them to suck them into his mouth. I squeezed my tit like I'd never touched it before in my life.

Hearing Jesse's voice on the phone was like going back in time, hearing the voices of boys I'd dated when I was a teenager and others I'd slept with when I was in my twenties and already considered to be an "older woman" by nineteen-year-olds. So much dead air between his sandpaper-voiced, "Hello," and awkward, "Oh...hi...hehe," after I told him who I was: the lady with the car.

"I'm still not one hundred percent sure, but I *might* be interested in selling you my car. Do you want to come over and give it a test drive?"

"Uhh...yeah! Yeah, definitely! Like in ten minutes? I can come over right now, that's perfect!"

His eagerness and ready availability made me laugh at the same time it made me feel like he was so close...like *I* was so close to having him. I reminded myself that while I was thinking about fucking him, he was only thinking about my car. I had no idea what was actually going to happen, if I could even interest him in something else. If I even should.

"Actually, noon tomorrow would be better...that way we'll have the roads to ourselves. We'll have to drive out of town if you really want to see how it runs."

"Yeah! Definitely! Okay, I'll come over at noon then, okay?"

I put on a simple sleeveless dress and cowboy boots and heard a knock five minutes early. Why did I feel so nervous? I opened the door and there he was, freshly shaven, his cheeks ruddy and lashes dark.

"Hi, Jesse! Thanks for being on time." I stepped toward him

briskly, all ready to go with my purse slung over my shoulder. He stepped aside just in time to get out of my way as I locked the door behind us, then led the way to the car while he followed behind me. I wondered if he was watching my ass or looking past me toward the real object of his desire: my car. With every step I took I was aware of my thighs brushing against each other and my lips feeling swollen and puffy above them. I wondered what Jesse's face would look like if I turned around and asked him if he wanted to drive my car or fuck my cunt.

I did turn around when I got to the car, a lewd grin on my face with the thought of the ridiculous proposition in my head and the awareness of how easy it would be to say it. All I had to do was open my mouth and possibly mortify both of us.

"Are you ready?" I asked as Jesse pulled something out of his pocket. He held his driver's license out to me in a formal manner, saying, "I just want you to know that I'm legal."

"Legal? For what?" I was still grinning and waited for him to answer before checking out his ID. *Tell me you're old enough to know how to use your nice big cock.*

"Uhh...legal to drive?" He blushed furiously, as though he could read my mind. Or maybe I'd read his. I think I was blushing too.

I opened the passenger door and held it open for him, explaining that I'd drive on our way out of town so I could tell him about some of the car's quirks, then he could drive on the way back. I didn't tell him that I'd picked out the exact spot where we could switch off or that I'd selected it for the privacy it provided. I told myself nothing was going to happen, but it would be fun to drive right up to the edge of what *could* happen so it would be even easier to fantasize "what if" later when it didn't.

Jesse hunkered down to get into the small, low-riding car. Standing above him gave me the perfect vantage point to check out his crotch in jeans, and the denim almost completely filled out around his muscular thighs. I loved the darker-blue wrinkles in the creases where his legs met his body. The moment was over too soon to gauge the size of his package properly, but just seeing the stiff ripples of bunched-up denim at his fly was enough to suggest promise.

I interrupted him when he fumbled for the shoulder belt, "It's automatic—you'll see it when I start up the car; just fasten your lap belt." He lifted his arms, looking down and all around, confused. I took the opportunity to bend and reach down beside him, pulling out the lap belt, and doing something a mother does for her child but with an entirely different intent; I inserted my upper body into the car to buckle him in, pulling the strap across his lap, making sure my knuckles didn't brush his pants, but allowing my hair to barely brush his face as I twisted my body in, holding onto the seat with my left hand, the heel resting on his bicep. My left breast grazed his chest briefly as I knew it would and my nipples pointed.

Click. "There you go!" I pretended to be in a motherly hurry while I inhaled his soap and sweat smell and imagined leaning closer toward him to feel his breath on my neck or losing my balance and somehow sitting in his lap; I wanted to, but didn't. Instead I put my right hand down on his knee for support. I estimated that I touched him for less than a second, then wondered how fast my car would be going if accelerated for just that amount of time. Ten miles per hour? Fifteen or twenty for the entire seatbelt performance?

I wanted to go faster.

While I started up the car I looked over at Jesse and the shoulder belt mechanically droning into place, trapping him. His hands sat like spiders on his thighs, resting on his fingertips like they were about to jump up and grab something. I put my hand on the stick shift and gave it a squeeze, imagining gripping his cock in the same way, wishing he'd move his hand to cover mine and add more pressure to the shaft inside our hands. He didn't, of course, so I pulled conservatively out on the road for some town driving. Like a safe ride in the car with Mommy down to the grocery store, only that's not where we were going. And I was no one's mommy.

Outside of town on a straight stretch, I decided to make sure the turbo still worked. The sudden rush of speed always made me laugh maniacally, especially after going such a long time without it. God, why didn't I drive that car every day? Climbing through the gears I felt shit dropping off behind me, leaving mundane crap all over the pavement like rubberized road apples shooting off in my wake. In fourth I got that buzzing feeling as we went faster, and faster, and faster, that I was about to meet the verge of something or crest and break completely free. It was like a flying dream. No, it was even better than a flying dream. I almost forgot about the kid next to me or maybe my inhibitions were part of the junk that second and third stroked away and I still felt him there, but wasn't afraid of being old next to him. I imagined my shiny rims flashing in the sun as I hovered between them, guiding the wheels and pushing things into place. I could move greased metal, I could turn things on; I could make things happen. I could even move myself from one place to another, fast. I left home behind and breathed speed straight through me.

I spilt into fifth and realized Jesse was clutching hard at the center console storage between us with his left hand while he wiped sweat from his other palm on his pant leg. I continued speeding for a few more seconds, enjoying the sound of passing obstacles, and placed my hand on his, yelling and squeezing for emphasis, "I DON'T KNOW IF I CAN SELL YOU MY CAR, JESSE!" Then I released my grip to slow and shift down to a more reasonable speed before turning onto a narrow, winding road.

The trees were dense and fully leafed out. There were no lines painted on this road, and I knew we probably wouldn't meet with much traffic, especially after a turn to the left and two turns to the right led us to a service road that would eventually turn to gravel. Right where pavement petered out into gravel is where I'd planned to stop.

Rocks crunched under my wide tires as I slowed to a halt. I didn't even bother turning around before stopping, not wanting to face the road back home yet. I clicked the ignition off, afraid again that I was being creepy, but enjoying the car's silence just the same and the way it amplified the sound of birds and tree leaves rustling. When Jesse didn't immediately open his door to change positions I was thankful. I decided to savor that moment sitting in a parked car with a teenaged boy—to freeze the feeling of nothing being over yet and everything smelling like fresh tree-moist air. Then the moment passed and my guts tightened with nervous energy. I was afraid if I didn't do something that I'd lose my chance. I unbuckled my lap belt trying to only move one arm but not the rest of my body, to demonstrate getting more comfortable in the car, but not getting out of it.

"It's a really nice day!" he said it a little too loud, like he was mimicking casual grown-up conversation. I was sure it wasn't the way he'd start a conversation with his friends, but I liked it because he was trying for something that wasn't about heading back home.

"What kind of music do you like?" he asked. "Is this a good tape?" He pushed the cassette into the player. It sprang into place. There was more silence and birds twittering.

I explained, "I have to turn the key to make it play." I turned the key then, and the screwy automatic shoulder belts lifted off our chests and purred up their tracks. The tape turned in the stereo, speakers only playing loops of static for a few revolutions at the songless end of one side before I turned it back off again. The belts ground back down to grip us. "Hey!" He laughed, perplexed.

"See? You don't want to buy this car anyway. The seat belts don't work right!" We laughed and he turned to me. "Maybe you should help me with my seat belt again."

Oh, my god.

First I unbuckled my own shoulder belt. Then I rested my elbow on the center console as I turned to him, feeling bubbles of fizz in my shook-up arms as I glided my left hand as steadily as I could across and down along the vinyl until I felt the button and released his lap belt. I let my hand keep moving then, onto his thigh, my fingers curling to the inside of his leg, mere millimeters from his balls. I didn't watch my hand, I watched his eyes and smelled the air turn into close-proximity about-to-kiss. I am going to know your mouth, Jesse.

I slid my hand slowly up the belt, making a smooth swipe from his hip and over his chest and shoulder, feeling the hot cotton of his T-shirt with my fingertips in contrast to the thick seat belt material under my palm. He watched my hand's progress with his mouth open, his hands gripping the seat, forearm muscles tensed. I lifted myself up to reach around him, unhooking his shoulder belt plugged in above his window, the softness of my right breast wobbling against his face, his mouth puffing hot air against it as he made a muffled "Oohgh" sound. He was like a well-trained boy at a titty bar resisting the urge to get handsy so he wouldn't be ejected.

By the time I sat back down my hand was on his thigh again. I looked down at my hand and picked the spot where I wanted it to go, slowly feeling for the hardness I knew was under the denim, reaching its resistance with my fingertips before pushing them over the hump, making a tunnel for it with my palm. He looked down at what I was doing to him, his mouth agape. I rubbed firmly down and back up, keeping my hand on his cock before I gave in, angling my body and aiming my mouth toward him with measured slowness in preparation to form a seal over his mouth.

When he realized I was about to kiss him, he must have accepted that the whole thing was real and he was allowed to take action because he suddenly grabbed at my tits with both hands, giving them a quick squeeze, then hastily decided he wanted my whole body. He grabbed me under the armpits and tried to hoist me onto him, but I wasn't prepared to assist with his efforts; my legs didn't make it over the hump and he lifted my head right into the roof of the car. Stymied, he went back to groping my tits, moving the fat in circles on my chest and moaning, "Come here...come here...get on top of me...."

I got on my knees, hoisting my dress up to my hips so he could see where my white panties cut up between my lips, and climbed onto him, my cowboy boots kicking and hanging up on the gearshift on the way over. Immediately he grabbed at my ass, stuffing his hands inside my panties down where I could feel his calloused hands squeezing fistfuls of my flesh while we kissed in famished gasps, Jesse sounding like a man having a nightmare about being really thirsty, sucking my tongue into his mouth. I lowered the seat back so fast our teeth clashed. There was so little space for four legs that I straddled just one of his, humping his thigh, rubbing my leg against his dick still trapped in his pants.

"Rub your pussy on my hand! Rub your pussy on my hand!" he gasped, and thrust his hand between me and his thigh, making his palm flat like holding it out for a dog to sniff to make it trust him. "I want to feel your pussy on my hand! Here, rub your pussy on my hand!" I did want to rub against his hand so with my panties barely hanging on in the front, I slid my clit along his whole hand, letting his crooked-up middle finger glide from my taint, to dipping wet cotton into my hole, and rubbing up over the shaft of my clit, up and down, my panties bunching up into wet wrinkles giving me even more to rub and wiggle against. I told him, "I want to touch you while I come. Take it out.... Lemme touch your cock!"

While he unbuttoned his fly in one fell swoop, I lifted and mashed my clit and puffy pussy lips against the heel of his hand, rubbing them all around on him while his middle finger searched around the opening of my underwear to squirm inside my cunt. He exposed his rigid prick by shoving his briefs down under his balls. We both fumbled at his cock while I kept humping him; by envisioning the hood of my clit crinkling and pushing back and forth over the shiny nub of my clit I felt it even more intensely, back and forth, until the rhythm of everything rubbing on my clit plus his squirming finger had me three rubs away. He guided my fingertips up and down the top of his cock and I started to come, unable to move my hand of my own volition so he moved it for me while I wailed, "OhYEAHyeahyeahyeah!" and he gasped, "Aagh! Aagh! Aagh!" as his come spurted onto our fingers. My hips ground in circles, winding down as I collapsed on top of him, his arms trapped under my body.

I asked him if he was ready to take the wheel and drive us back, and when he confessed, "I don't actually know how to drive a stick," I lifted my head in time to see him grin at me and add, "but I was hoping you'd like to teach me later."

ABOUT THE AUTHORS

KRIS ADAMS works in the library sciences field and has been writing erotic fan fiction since her teens.

VALERIE ALEXANDER is a freelance writer currently at work on her first collection of erotica. She resides in Arizona with her long-term partner.

JACQUELINE APPLEBEE is a black British woman, who breaks down barriers with smut. Jacqueline's stories have appeared in *Iridescence: Sensuous Shades of Lesbian Erotica; Travelrotica for Lesbians Volume 2; Best Women's Erotica 2008;* and *Best Lesbian Erotica 2008.* She also has a paranormal novella entitled *Fallen Soldiers* that includes sex with ghosts! Her website is at writing-in-shadows.co.uk.

JANINE ASHBLESS's erotica debut was with a collection of short fantasy, fairy, and paranormal stories, *Cruel Enchantment,* published by Black Lace in 2000. The follow-up volume to this collection is scheduled for 2009. In between, she has written three erotic fantasy novels for Black Lace: *Divine Torment, Burning Bright,* and *Wildwood.* Her first story for Cleis appeared in *I Is for Indecent.* Her website is janineashbless.com.

CHEYENNE BLUE combines her two passions in life and writes travel guides and erotica. Her erotica has appeared in several anthologies, including *Best Women's Erotica, Mammoth Best New Erotica, Best Lesbian Erotica, Best Lesbian Love Stories,* and on many websites. Her travel guides have been jammed into many glove boxes underneath the chocolate wrappers. She divides her time between Colorado, USA, and Ireland, and is currently working on a book about the quiet and quirky areas of Ireland. You can see more of her erotica on her website, cheyenneblue.com.

DEBORAH CASTELLANO graduated from Douglass College with a degree in women's studies in 2001. Since then, she has been an executive administrator by day and head of her convention, SalonCon by night. She has written for *Venus, SageWoman,* and *NewWitch* magazines.

ELIZABETH COLDWELL is the editor of the UK edition of *Forum* magazine. Her stories have appeared in numerous anthologies including *Best Women's Erotica 2006; Best S/M Erotica 1* and *2; Yes, Sir;* and *Spanked: Red-Cheeked Erotica.*

TRIXIE FONTAINE makes autobiographical pornography at home with her trans girlfriend. She's been blogging since 2001 and broadcasting voyeurcams on TastyTrixie.com since 2002. The latest feather in her cap is her Twitter account (twitter.com/tastytrixie) where she keeps everyone posted on her dreams and the frequency of her bowel movements. This is her first submission to a collection of erotica; she hopes it will be met with as much enthusiasm as her excretory tweets. You can read her nonfiction piece, "Menstruation: Porn's Last Taboo," in *Best Sex Writing 2008*. In between shooting nudie pics, she works on writing her first novel: the deliciously tawdry *Ms. Trixie's Rooming House for Emancipated Girls.*

SCARLETT FRENCH's erotic fiction has appeared in *Lipstick on Her Collar; Best Women's Erotica 2008; Fantasy: Untrue Stories of Lesbian Passion; Best Women's Erotica 2007; Tales of Travelrotica for Lesbians; First-Timers: True Stories of Lesbian Awakening; Best Lesbian Erotica 2005;* and *Va Va Voom*. Having procrastinated for long enough on her first novel, she has decided to instead write an erotic novel, in the hope of getting past chapter four.

ELISA GARCIA is a freelance writer and Latin dance enthusiast. A corporate America refugee, she now works at home and lives with her partner and child outside of Houston.

D. L. KING pens smut from somewhere between the Wonder Wheel and the Chrysler Building. Some of her latest short stories can be found in *Best Lesbian Erotica 2008; Yes, Ma'am: Erotic Stories of Male Submission; Yes, Sir: Erotic Stories of Female Submission,* and *Frenzy: 60 Stories of Sudden Sex.*

Her novels, *The Melinoe Project* and *The Art of Melinoe,* can be found at Renaissance E Books. D. L. King is the editor of the review site, Erotica Revealed. Visit the author at dlkingerotica.com.

SOMMER MARSDEN's work has appeared in numerous print anthologies. Some of her favorites include, *Love at First Sting, I Is for Indecent, J Is for Jealousy, Ultimate Lesbian Erotica 2008, Whip Me, Spank Me,* and *Yes, Sir.* She lives, works, and pens smut from her small home in her small town. She is an Internet junkie who is addicted to procrastination and Sprees. You can keep track of her many misadventures by visiting Smut-Girl.blogspot.com.

KAY JAYBEE has had a number of stories published in Cleis Press anthologies (*Lips Like Sugar, Best Women's Erotica 2007, Lust, Best Women's Erotica 2008)*, and *Sex and Music*, *Ultimate Sin*, and *The Mammoth Book of Lesbian Erotica.* She is also a regular contributor to the erotic website Oysters & Chocolate, and her story "Tied to the Kitchen Sink" is featured as a podcast on Violet Blue's Open Source Sex. Kay is very much looking forward to the publication of her first solo work of erotica, *The Collector* (Austin & Macauley), which will be available in late 2008.

JANNE LEWIS is new to the field of erotic writing but has been published in other genres. She has always had vivid and detailed erotic fantasies, and with her husband's encouragement began writing them down. She has worked in the past as a waitress, a lawyer, and a stay-at-home mom.

Ms. Naughty is a writer, editor, blogger, and online pornographer with a passion for women's erotica. She began her literary career writing stories and articles for *Australian Women's Forum* and the *Sydney Morning Herald* in the late '90s. Since 2000 she has built a stable of adult websites for women including MsNaughty.com. She also co-owns ForTheGirls.com, a large paysite and online magazine and regularly writes and edits stories, reviews, and articles for the site. She has also overseen three annual erotic fiction competitions for FTG. She lives with her husband in a small Australian town, surrounded by Fundamentalist Christians.

Donna George Storey's erotic fiction has appeared in more than sixty journals and anthologies including Clean Sheets, Fishnet, *Best American Erotica 2006, Mammoth Book of Best New Erotica,* and her very favorite place to hang with great dirty-story writers, *Best Women's Erotica.* Her novel, *Amorous Woman,* the story of an American woman's love affair with Japan and her steamy encounters with sexy men and women along the way, was published by Orion in 2007. She currently writes a column "Cooking Up a Storey" for the Erotica Readers and Writers Association. Read more of her work at DonnaGeorgeStorey.com.

Vanessa Vaughn is a twentysomething currently living in Dallas with her husband. After pursuing a short but successful career in fundraising for the arts, she is now devoting herself to what she loves best: writing. Some of the many things that turn her on include vampires, tennis skirts, long cigarettes, any woman from a Wachowski brothers movie, tattoos, Southern gentlemen, uni, gold bullion, Stephen Colbert, WOW geeks, burlesque, and fine wine, in no particular order. This is her first published work.

ALANA NOËL VOTH's writing has appeared in *The Mammoth Book of Best New Erotica Volume 7; Best Gay Erotica 2008, 2007,* and *2004; Best Gay Bondage Erotica; Best American Erotica 2005; Best Bisexual Women's Erotica; Where the Boys Are: Urban Gay Erotica; I Is for Indecent;* and online at Literary Mama, Big Stupid Review, Cleansheets, Eclectica Magazine, and Oysters and Chocolate.

XAN WEST is the pseudonym of a New York City BDSM and sex educator and writer. Xan's work can be found in *Best Women's Erotica 2008, Best S/M Erotica Volume 2, Got a Minute?, Love at First Sting,* and the forthcoming *Hurts So Good* and *M Is for Master.* Xan has a particular love for belts, biting, public sex, and boots. Xan wants to hear from you and can be reached at xan_west@yahoo.com.

LAUREN WRIGHT is perhaps the only cognitive neuroscientist who has ever wondered why she didn't become a professional dominatrix instead. An overstressed and overworked doctoral student, she would be classified by most who know her as a good girl who lives life by the rules, but in her spare time she is very, very bad. "On Loan" is her first published piece of erotica. She lives and writes in her hometown of Ottawa, Ontario.

New to writing erotica, LUX ZAKARI has been published on the website Oysters & Chocolate (www.oystersandchocolate.com). She's currently working on a full-length erotic novel about bad boys corrupting good girls in the 1970s.

ABOUT THE EDITOR

Violet Blue is a Forbes Web Celeb and one of *Wired*'s 2008 "Faces of Innovation." She is a widely known blogger, podcaster, reporter, and fembot at Geek Entertainment Television and Gawker Media's Fleshbot. She is the *San Francisco Chronicle's* sex columnist, and Blue writes about sexuality for outlets such as *Forbes* and *O: The Oprah Magazine*. She lectures to cyberlaw classes at UC Berkeley, tech conferences, and sex crisis counselors at community teaching institutions. Her podcast is the notorious Open Source Sex and her tech blog is techyum.com. Blue self-publishes DRM-free audio and ebooks at DigitaPublications.com.

Blue has authored and edited over two dozen published books and contributed to five nonfiction books from other authors). Blue has been interviewed and featured prominently by major publications and media outlets including *Wired*, *Newsweek*, MSNBC, the *Wall Street Journal*, NPR, BoingBoing.net (viewable at violetblueviolet blue.net), Salon.com, BBC, CNN, the *New York Times*, About.com, PBS, CBS, The History Channel, *Esquire*, *Jane*, *Maxim*, *Marie Claire*, and many more, including more magazines, newspapers, and major city weeklies ranging from the *Village Voice* and the *SF Bay Guardian* to appearances in "Savage Love." Her popular personal website is TinyNibbles.com.